We Own the Sky

ALSO BY RODMAN PHILBRICK

Freak the Mighty

Max the Mighty

The Fire Pony

REM World

The Last Book in the Universe

The Young Man and the Sea

The Mostly True Adventures of Homer P. Figg

Zane and the Hurricane: A Story of Katrina

The Big Dark

Who Killed Darius Drake?: A Mystery

Wildfire

*Stay Alive: The Journal of Douglas Allen Deeds,
The Donner Party Expedition, 1846*

Wild River

We Own the Sky

RODMAN PHILBRICK

Scholastic Press

New York

Library of Congress Cataloging-in-Publication Data available

ISBN 978-1-338-73629-8

10 9 8 7 6 5 4 3 2 1   22 23 24 25 26

Printed in the U.S.A.   37
First edition, September 2022

Book design by Elizabeth B. Parisi

For Paul Bamberger,
friend, poet, and fellow reader

This was the year the men in white robes and pointy hoods infected the great state of Maine, and made so many of us stupid and hateful, and others rise as heroes to oppose them. It was also the year my sister walked on wings. It was a time of astonishing courage, a time of betrayal and disaster, a time of derring-do, when girls and boys thought nothing of stepping into the clear blue sky.

I'll never forget, old as I am, because I remember it like yesterday . . .

June 21, 1924
Biddeford, Maine

1. *In Which Our Fortunes Change*

ASIDE FROM THE priest and the gravediggers, me and
my sister, Jo, are the only ones to witness our dear mother,
Eva Morin Michaud, being lowered into her grave. Papa
having perished in a mill accident some years previously,
the hard, hard loss of our mama makes us orphans.

When I begin to cuss the lung ailment that so cruelly
took her from us, Jo hushes me.

"Wait until the priest is out of earshot," she says, hugging me tight. "Then I shall join you, and we'll cuss like
pirates. We'll turn the air blue, Davy, I promise."

I won't put down what we said, exactly, for fear it'll
set this page on fire. First, I cussed the illness, then I cussed
the cotton dust that gave her the illness, then I cussed the
mill foreman for not letting our mother's many friends
attend her burial, it being a workday. I vowed that he

should fall through the floor of a stinking outhouse, and be buried up to his neck until his odor improved, if ever it did. Then Jo took to cussing the run of bad luck that has got the best of us, and may end with me in a home for little wanderers, which I dread more than anything.

We cuss like sailors, but no, we do not take our Lord's name in vain. Mama, who never missed Mass, would not approve of such a thing. When, finally, we run out of steam, Jo has tears in her eyes and I'm blubbering like a baby.

"Don't worry, little brother," Jo says. "I have a plan. I will quit school and apply for Mama's job, or one like it."

"You'll do no such thing! You must go on to teachers' college, like you always wanted. It's me who'll quit school. The nuns would have me sent to what they call a boarding school for boys, but that's just another name for a Sisters of Mercy orphanage. No way! I'll take a factory job instead. They'll have me as a mill monkey, on account of my size."

Mill monkeys are what some call the children who work in and around the belts and spinners that power the great looms. It is dangerous work, and Jo does not approve of any child laboring, let alone me. Her face gets stony and her tears dry up. She's about to point a finger in my face and tell me off when at that very moment a horn honks twice, as if to get our attention.

A grand, gleaming red automobile makes a turn onto the graveyard road. It's a Cadillac V-63, which I've been mooning over in the advertisements. The beautiful machine comes to a stop not ten feet from us, and out leaps an athletic young woman dressed in formal black, carrying flowers.

"Oh dear! Have I missed it?"

We've never met, but I recognize her from the newspapers and magazines. Those high cheekbones and wide-apart eyes. It is Ruthie Reynard, our mother's famous cousin. Record-setting aviatrix, and star of her very own flying circus.

"Come here, children," Ruthie says, striding to the grave. "We have much to discuss."

I gulp and reach for my sister's hand.

2. What "Tour" Means

THE FAMOUS FEMALE flyer tenderly places the flowers on Mama's grave, then makes the sign of the cross.

"Now to the business at hand." She snaps open her purse. "No, I said it wrong. Not business, but family."

She takes an envelope from the purse. "Your mother wrote to me recently, asking would I see to it that you were cared for after her death. How could I decline? Besides, by the time her letter arrived, she was already gone."

Something about Ruthie's tone makes Jo defiant. "We can take care of ourselves," she insists.

Ruthie studies her for a moment and smiles thoughtfully. "Yes, of course you can. On an entirely different subject, I am famished. I noticed a diner down the road. Would you join me for a bite to eat?"

The ride to the diner is my first in such a grand vehicle. I hope it will not be my last.

———

Ruthie says we can order anything we like, and we settle on pancakes and eggs and sausage and maple syrup and milk cold from the icebox. Soon as the food arrives I get busy laying waste to the pancakes. Truth is, Jo and I have not been eating much lately. They stopped Mama's pay the day she fell ill with coughing, and we're down to crumbs and heated water that we pretend is soup.

Jo has her head down, working on eggs and toast and a heap of sausage. Nobody says much, because we're so busy chewing. Except for Ruthie, who pushes a little sandwich around her plate.

It strikes me she fibbed about being hungry as an excuse to feed us.

"As children, your mother and I were thick as thieves," she says. "We were *petite-cousine*, distant cousins. Speaking mostly French, we were that young. This was in Lewiston. When Eva's father moved the family to Biddeford for a better job, we lost touch."

Jo groans and pushes her plate away. "One more bite and I'll bust."

Ruthie touches the letter. "This was the first I'd heard from her since we were about your age, Davy. You're, what, twelve?"

I nod. Grateful she hasn't yet mentioned me being small for my age, as many do.

"I had no idea she had married, had children, and been widowed so young," Ruthie says, marveling at the sad surprise. "I am so sorry for your loss, but here I am, to make sure you are properly situated."

Properly situated? I'm not sure I like the sound of that.

"As I see it, we have two choices. Either you remain in Biddeford, under the care of your parish priest, or you can tour with me for the season."

"What does *tour* mean?" Jo wants to know.

Ruthie smiles. "It means you'll join my flying circus."

3. *I Fly Tomorrow*

AT FIRST JO resists the notion, because at seventeen she's nearly an adult. But really, it's pure Michaud stubbornness—Jo has been in charge of caring for dear Mama, and now she wants to be in charge of her own self.

Ruthie has the sense to treat Jo like a grown-up, even if she hasn't quite turned eighteen.

"I'm not offering a handout," the famous aviatrix explains, sounding as prim as a schoolmarm. "Certainly not for sentimental reasons. Truth is, we can use the help. Josephine, you will be in charge of ticketing, collecting cash, and seeing it counted and locked in the safe. Your salary, three dollars per show. Davy, you'll sell popcorn and make a penny profit on every nickel. By season's end your circumstances will have improved considerably."

"Oh my," says Jo, eyes bright with approval.

I'd bet my life she's already counting the money in her mind. Me, I'm spending my penny profits on a brand-new baseball mitt like some of the bigger kids have. A Spalding or maybe a Wilson.

"It's settled, then," Ruthie says, rising from the table and pulling on her gloves. *"Très bien, mes amis.* Very good, my friends. We'll collect your things and be on our way. I fly tomorrow."

———

I'll never forget the splendid ride from Biddeford to Waterville, perched in the brown leather seats of Ruthie's Cadillac V-63. She drives with both hands firmly on the wheel, her large eyes never straying from the road ahead. Ruthie Reynard is a renowned daredevil of the air and holds the record for loop the loops by any flier, man or woman. Something tells me that if Jo and I weren't along, she'd be going a lot faster.

It seems like a dream that this famous lady has swooped in to help us, if only for the summer. Our dear mama kept scrapbooks of Ruthie's exploits, clipped from newspapers and magazines, but never would reach out to her childhood friend. Some of that was pride, not wanting her cousin to know how low we had fallen after Papa died. Some of it was fear, I think, that Ruthie would not remember her from those days so long ago.

What terrible rotten luck that Mama cannot be here! Doubtless she is looking down from heaven with a big smile, but it doesn't stop the hurt of losing her. Jo squeezes my hand as if she's reading my thoughts, which sometimes she can do better than a fortune-teller. "It's okay to be sad and excited at the same time," she whispers.

The road to Waterville is partway paved, but as we approach the fairgrounds, it goes back to gravel, and the tires make it sound like the ocean, although we are miles from the sea. I get up on my knees in the back seat for a better view, and that's when I see my first ever airplane, tipping wings as it passes over us on the way to the landing field.

"That will be Captain Merriman," Ruthie says. "The best aviator in the show, other than me, of course."

As we drive over the top of a hill, the whole fairground comes into view. There are two more planes—Jenny biplanes!—parked side by side, and a Bugatti Brescia Grand Prix race car, and a motorcycle, and a row of good-sized tents, and a *Ruthie Reynard's Flying Circus* banner rippling in the breeze.

Ruthie pulls up to the tents.

"Welcome to your summer home," she says with a grin.

4. *An Element of Danger*

I DO NOT know where, exactly, I expected us to stay as we moved from place to place with the air show. At grand hotels, maybe? Grand hotels with wide verandas, and well-dressed guests wandering about, and little handbells to ring for service. Whatever I was expecting, it wasn't tents! Not that I have anything against tents, mind you, and it turns out these have all the homey touches, fitted out with comfortable furniture and oil lamps, and nice rugs to tickle your bare feet! Sleeping cots are divided off by curtains, for privacy.

The men have one tent and the ladies another, with one exception. Me. For the time being, Ruthie insists I stay with her and Jo.

"A child who has just lost his mother needs to be with family. Later you can bunk with the men, but for now, I'm keeping you close to your big sister."

I don't like being called a child, not one bit. I may be small for my age (not yet five foot tall, try as I might to grow some), but I don't want her thinking I'm a little kid, or treating me like one. I open my mouth to object, then think better of it. There's only one boss of Ruthie Reynard's Flying Circus, and that's Ruthie herself. The US Army gave her an honorary captain's rank and a military uniform for her help selling war bonds. Epaulets on her shoulders, a tunic with two rows of buttons, jodhpur riding trousers, and knee-high black boots polished to a mirror finish. An outfit like that makes me want to salute, but Ruthie forbids it.

"It is only a costume," she insists. "I must look the part. So must each of you when you're part of the team. The aviators and stuntmen and stuntwomen are the stars, but none of it happens without ground support."

Jo's eyes widen. "Stuntwomen?"

"Lily Bash, wing walker," Ruthie says with a grin. "Does that appeal, the notion of a female daredevil?"

Jo suddenly goes quiet and shrugs.

"You'll meet Lily tomorrow, and all the crew. Today I want you to rest up, get your air legs."

"Air legs?" I ask.

"Sailors have sea legs, a sense of balance that allows

them to walk on a rolling deck. Aviators have air legs, so we always know where we are, even if we're flying upside down. We fly upside down a *lot*. Audiences love it, and the closer to the ground the better."

Jo's eyes are enormous. "Sounds dangerous," she says, her voice catching.

Ruthie's smile is replaced by a stern look. "Yes. Correct. Everything we do has an element of danger. If it wasn't dangerous and thrilling, no one would pay to see us. Don't look so shocked, young lady. We take all precautions. I don't deny we've had a few accidents, but no lives have been lost. The day that happens is the day I quit. Understood?"

We both say yes.

"To bed!"

That night, on my new cot, in this strange new world of flying machines and daredevils, I dream the cot has biplane wings and carries me high over the fairgrounds. I am wonderfully afraid, but the sky is a happy place and I wish never to touch the sad earth again.

I miss Mama so much it hurts.

5. *Winged Bullets*

MOST FAIRGROUNDS HAVE a dirt racetrack, and this one is no exception. Ruthie chose the location to kick off her statewide tour because of the ample grandstands, which can hold two thousand spectators on wooden planks. She seats us in the highest row, looking down on the finish line.

"I want you to experience the entire show exactly as the spectators see it, from first to last. Starting tomorrow you'll be working with the ground crew and won't always have time to look up."

Before leaving to ready her aircraft, she gives us coins for peanuts and popcorn and tells us to enjoy ourselves. Not that we need to be encouraged! Just being in a crowd this size is exciting. The first show kicks off at one o'clock, and by then almost every seat is occupied.

Raised up behind us on a little platform is the show announcer, a burly man with a big bow tie, shouting into a mounted megaphone that's bigger than he is.

"LADIES AND GENTLEMEN! KIDS OF ALL AGES! PREPARE YOURSELVES! WHAT YOU ARE ABOUT TO SEE MAY SHOCK YOU TO THE CORE! YOU WILL WITNESS DEATH-DEFYING FEATS OF DERRING-DO! YOU WILL SEE FLYING MACHINES AND RACE CARS AND MOTORCYCLES WHOSE SPEED EXCEEDS ONE HUNDRED MILES PER HOUR! YOU WILL WITNESS THRILLING STUNTS PERFORMED BY AMERICA'S FAVORITE AVIATRIX, THE FIRST PILOT OF ANY GENDER TO FLY NONSTOP BETWEEN CHICAGO AND NEW YORK! THE FIRST PILOT TO FLY UPSIDE DOWN UNDER THE BROOKLYN BRIDGE! HOLDER OF THE RECORD FOR MOST LOOP THE LOOPS! LADIES AND GENTLEMEN, CAST YOUR EYES TO THE EAST! I GIVE YOU RUTHIE REYNARD'S FLYING CIRCUS!"

Seemingly out of nowhere, two Curtiss Jenny biplanes zoom up over the edge of the opposite grandstand. They look close enough to reach out and touch. The planes roll and separate and then head straight at me and Jo. Flying machines with great whirring propellers.

Propellers that could take off our heads, if the pilots make a mistake.

They aim for us like winged bullets. Coming so fast we couldn't get out of the way even if we wanted to, packed into the stands as we are. Ruthie, grinning beneath her goggles, pulls up at the last possible instant. The wind from the prop knocks me to my knees. I manage to turn around and see both pilots waving merrily at us from their cockpits.

I've never been so scared, but the funny thing is, I can't wait to do it again.

———

The announcer stands at his giant megaphone, shouting out what happens next.

"LADIES AND GENTLEMEN! BEHOLD ONE OF THE FASTEST RACING AUTOMOBILES IN THE WORLD! THE BUGATTI TYPE 35, DRIVEN BY FAMED ITALIAN DAREDEVIL TONY MARTINI! NOTHING CAN BEAT THE BUGATTI AROUND THE TRACK! OR CAN IT?"

The race car roars onto the track, with the driver half standing behind the wheel so he can wave at the crowd as he passes the grandstands. With his thick black hair and chiseled profile, he looks a little like Valentino, the film star. Martini drops into the seat and guns the eight-cylinder engine. The sleek vehicle accelerates like a fireworks rocket, sliding into the first turn, barely under control.

Or maybe the driver wants us to think he's out of control. All part of the show. I'm about to tug on Jo's sleeve and ask what she thinks when Ruthie's biplane swoops over the racetrack and starts chasing the Bugatti. At first it almost looks like she's going to land on the track, she's that close to the ground. We're actually looking down on her as she zooms by the grandstands.

How magnificent she looks with her goggles and leather earflaps, and her white silk scarf rippling in the wind!

At the first turn the biplane banks, nearly cutting into the dirt with the tips of its wings. The race car scoots ahead, sliding through the turn. Ruthie levels her wings, increasing her speed, and passes the Bugatti on the inside of the second turn.

Again and again, the biplane wingtips almost skim the dirt. If they hit, the plane will spin out of control and crash for sure. My heart is slamming so hard I can barely breathe. The race is exciting, but not as horribly thrilling as the possibility that brave Ruthie Reynard is risking death by flying so close to the ground.

Jo must feel the same way. If her eyes get any bigger, they'll fall out of her head.

The Jenny and the Italian race car roar down the homestretch neck and neck, fighting for the lead. As they cross the finish line the biplane pulls ahead by a nose, or, as the announcer shouts, "THE THICKNESS OF A PROPELLER BLADE!"

I'm ready to sit down and catch my breath, but the show has barely begun.

6. *Crazy Wonderful Acts of Courage*

THE STUNTS BECOME even more wild and dangerous. Captain Ray Merriman, racing ahead of two men on a motorcycle, drops a rope ladder from his biplane. A man—Tony Martini again—leaps from the back of the motorcycle, grabs the rope ladder, and climbs up onto the bottom wing. He shakes hands with the pilot, waves at the roaring crowd, and pretends to blow kisses. Then, casual as can be, he flips down from the bottom wing to the landing gear. Spreading wide his arms, he hangs upside down from the wheel axle like a trapeze artist, with nothing to hold him but the strength of his legs.

I have to close my eyes and take a breath. Surely, he will slip from the axle and plunge to the ground.

"LADIES AND GENTS!" the announcer bellows.

"CAST YOUR EYES TO THE GENTLEMAN WITH THE HAT! WATCH CAREFULLY, BECAUSE SEEING IS BELIEVING!"

Down on the track a tall, slender man lifts his black bowler hat and waves it at the crowd. Some in the stands cheer—maybe they know what is about to happen—while the rest of us can only guess.

The man holds the hat as high as he can. Waiting.

Could it be? No, impossible!

Captain Merriman's Jenny is flying about a hundred feet from the ground, with Tony Martini hanging upside down from the axle. The biplane slows until it looks like it might fall from the sky. Then it takes direct aim at the man with the upheld hat.

The Jenny flies lower and lower. Impossibly, dangerously low.

Will the man with the hat stand his ground, or turn and flee from the deadly propeller?

He stands like a statue. Motionless, waiting. The Jenny sinks lower and lower, engine sputtering. The daredevil can't be more than six feet above the ground, hanging upside down by his knees, hands outstretched.

If the biplane doesn't veer away, man and machine will collide.

The crowd hushes. Can they survive, the pilot, the daredevil, the man with the hat? Will the Jenny sink too low? Will the stunt end in tragedy?

I want to cover my eyes, I really do. But, somehow, I can't. And then, in an instant, it's over. The Jenny rises ever so slightly and dangling Tony Martini grabs the hat as the man deftly falls away, avoiding the propeller and the landing gear.

We all leap to our feet, roaring our relief.

"Jo! Jo! Did you see that?"

My big sister doesn't answer. I'm not sure she even hears me, so entranced is she with the flying circus. The machines, the stunts, the crazy, wonderful acts of courage. She has a dreamy look of surprise on her face, as if she's discovered something unexpected.

Something she never knew she wanted.

7. Men with Torches

ACCORDING TO RUTHIE, the final show of the day—by now it is evening—is less about risky stunts and more about fireworks.

"The point is to make it look dangerous when in fact what we're doing is quite safe," she reassures us.

By "we" she means herself and Captain Ray Merriman, each flying a Curtiss JN-4, better known as a Jenny. The fabric-covered fuselages have been illuminated from within so that the audience can see the airplanes in the gathering dusk. They look like giant lightning bugs swooping above the grandstands. Ruthie and the captain stage an aerial "dogfight," diving at each other as if in combat, pulling away at the last possible moment.

Instead of machine guns, they fire Roman candles from their cockpits.

"What if they catch fire?" I ask Jo.

She pats my hand reassuringly. "Not to worry, Davy. The Jennys have been equipped with fire extinguishers. Ruthie says they've never had a serious fire. Not one they couldn't put out."

In the grand finale of the evening show, the two illuminated biplanes fly through a barrage of fireworks launched from the middle of the track. Close enough so the breeze blows sparks our way, as well as the sweet scent of exploded gunpowder. Sweet to me because I love fireworks, especially the ones that bloom like red and blue flowers. Ruthie and Captain Merriman seem to be in the midst of the explosions, but Jo explains that it's partly an illusion. They're flying close to the line of skyrockets, but not directly through it.

"They don't take crazy chances," Jo says with great confidence. "It's all about putting on a good show without getting hurt."

"You think it's safe to hang upside down from the axle with your head between the propeller and the ground?"

I can feel Jo's disapproval. "It is if you're a trained athlete like Tony Martini, and your pilot is Ray Merriman," she insists.

"You know a lot about it."

"I'm learning," she says firmly. "This will be our life for

the next few months, Davy. We can't do our part if we're scared every stunt will end badly."

"I'm not scared."

"Good, then." She gives my shoulder a squeeze.

That was a lie. The idea of daredevils risking their lives is deeply disturbing. How do they do it? How can they be so brave? I could never be like that. I'm much too small to be a hero. That's my secret and no one can know, not even Jo.

Especially Jo.

The fireworks have ended and the biplanes have landed safely. The fuselage illumination has been turned off. The crowd streams out of the grandstands to their automobiles and their horses and wagons.

"Come on, little brother. They'll be expecting us."

As I stand up something catches my eye. "Jo, what's that? Through the trees in that other pasture, do you see?"

Trees separate the fairgrounds from a hillside pasture and partially block a line of flickering lights that caught my eye. Flames. Is it a brush fire? The grass set alight by a skyrocket?

Wanting to see more clearly, I clamber up the steps to the announcer's platform. Jo is right behind me, ducking under the huge megaphone to get a better view.

"Torches," she says. "Hoods and torches. They're having a parade."

8. *What Hateful Men Believe*

JO AND I are headed for that nearby field, to investigate the torch-lit parade, when Ruthie looms out of the twilight and halts us in our tracks.

"I saw them from the air, streaming onto the hillside. Men who cover their faces and march into the night with flaming torches are up to no good. Best steer clear, understood?"

"Yes, ma'am."

"Good. Please join us in the canteen."

The canteen is an army-style tent set up with portable stoves and griddles, and folding tables and chairs. Oil lamps give it a warm glow. As we enter, wonderful smells make my mouth water. The cook is Mrs. Mangano. Maggie. She has a heavy Italian accent, and as soon as she spots me in line, holding an empty plate out, she decides to save me from starvation. "*Magro il figlio!* You a skinny one! Maggie fix that!"

I decide not to fight it. Besides, I'm starving and the food smells strange and delicious, and everybody in the canteen tent is happy in an eager kind of way. That's as good as a full stomach, in my opinion. I've never been in the company of so many happy, contented people, and for that I am truly grateful.

If the famous aviatrix hadn't showed up, Jo and I would be out on the street. Evicted from the mill-owned tenement because Mama no longer worked there. Instead we're stuffing ourselves near to bursting on food we've never heard of: pasta e fagioli (macaroni soup), pancetta (sort of like bacon), cotoletta di pollo (the most amazing fried chicken cutlets), and heavenly, cream-filled pastries called cannoli.

After the feast, I work up the courage to ask Ruthie about the mysterious torchlight parade. "Who are they? What are they doing?"

She sighs and makes a face. "It was a rally, I believe. A hate rally. An excuse to spout lies and practice cruelty. I mean it, Davy, stay away from men like that. We have free speech in this country, so they can spew whatever poison they want, but we don't have to listen."

It feels like there's more she's not telling me. The

way grown-ups do who think I'm not old enough to understand. But she makes it clear that the conversation is over, as far as she's concerned, and that's that.

I'll ask Jo about it later.

———

"Ku Klux Klan," my sister explains. "The KKK. In the South they lynch and murder Blacks with impunity. Their hatred has spread far beyond the South. They have infested Maine, and since there are so few dark-skinned people in the state, the main target of their rage is people like us."

We're seated at the small folding card table in our tent, in the flickering light of an oil lamp that is about to run out of fuel. Whispering between us, because others are sleeping, and because discussion of the subject has been discouraged.

Too scary for a boy my age, or so they think.

"What do you mean, 'people like us'?"

Jo shrugs. "Folks who came down from Quebec to work in the mills and brought the French language with them, like our papa. Or the Italian language, or the Polish language, or Yiddish, or any language other than English. The Maine Klansmen despise immigrants, especially Catholic or Jewish immigrants. They believe we have invaded their country, and that the white race and their way of life will be overwhelmed."

"That's stupid," I say.

"That's what makes them so dangerous. Mix ignorance with fear, and bad things happen. Ruthie is right to tell us to steer clear of the Klan. Time for bed, little brother. We join the ground crew at dawn."

I lie awake for a long while, staring up at the center pole of the tent, thinking about things. The town we left behind, and our dear parents who are together again in heaven, and what will become of us after our time with the circus is over. Enough things to make my head feel swollen, and heavy upon the thin pillow.

When sleep comes at last I dream we're running uphill, Jo and me, fleeing from the light of torches.

9. *Hold Fast or Die*

THE NEXT DAY we are put to work. Jo goes off with Ruthie to learn about selling tickets and looking after the cash. Meanwhile, Mrs. Mangano shows me how to make popcorn in a big iron kettle. Pour a bag of hard kernels into the simmering cooking oil, slide the heavy cover in place, and wait for the corn to start popping. Sounds like a gun battle inside the kettle. The secret is to swing the kettle away from the fire just as the last kernel pops, so the unpopped kernels on the bottom don't burn.

It's up to me to scoop the hot popcorn into waxed paper bags, add melted butter and salt. The bags are stacked in a canvas carrier that loops over my neck and around my waist. That way my hands are free to pass out the bags and collect the nickels.

So much popcorn! So many nickels!

The grandstands begin to fill when the gates open, an hour before the first show. There are vendors selling hot dogs and bottles of soda pop, but it seems like everybody wants popcorn. I'm so busy passing bags and waiting for the nickels to come back that I almost miss Ruthie's red Cadillac arriving in a cloud of road dust. Tony Martini leaps out of the driver's seat and opens the rear door. Out steps a stylish young girl with bobbed dark hair who waves cheerfully to the applauding crowd.

Not a girl, but a very small woman, not much taller than me. Under five feet tall. Someone in the stands shouts, "Lily, I love you!" and then they're all chanting "Lill-ee, Lill-ee, Lill-ee!"

Must be Lily Bash, the famous wing walker. She's been away on some family matter, so Jo and I haven't met her yet. Tony must have picked her up at the train station in Waterville and brought her to the fairgrounds for a grand entrance.

"LILL-EE, LILL-EE, LILL-EE!"

The tiny woman takes a deep bow, salutes her fans, and strides off with daredevil Tony Martini, no doubt to get ready for the show.

Do wing walkers wear parachutes in case they fall? I decide to ask Ruthie when I get the chance, and then I'm so busy making and selling popcorn I almost forget about Lily Bash.

Almost, but not quite.

The air show is exactly the same as yesterday except Tony fails to grab the tall man's hat on the first try. Or maybe they missed on purpose to make the second attempt all the more exciting and suspenseful. Yes, that's it, because this time when the Jenny swoops low with Tony hanging from the landing gear, the man with the hat TURNS HIS BACK TO THE APPROACHING BIPLANE. Turns his back to the deadly propeller! Surely it will strike him dead if he does not move. The man holds the hat as high as he can reach. Somehow, he falls away at exactly the right moment and Tony has the hat in his hands and the Jenny swoops up, wagging wings, and the crowd—and me, too— roars approval.

"Popcorn! Hey, popcorn over here!"

Back to work. Every bag sold earns me a penny. It adds up—already I've made almost a dollar and it's only the first show. I'm down to the last bag or two, almost time to head down for a new batch, when the announcer stops me in my tracks.

"LADIES AND GENTLEMEN! ATTENTION, PLEASE! YOU ARE ABOUT TO WITNESS THE MOST DANGEROUS STUNT IN ALL OF AVIATION! MANY

HAVE PERISHED IN THE ATTEMPT! PRAY THEIR NUMBER SHALL NOT INCREASE TODAY! CAST YOUR EYES TO THE EAST! LOOK SHARP TO THE EAST! I GIVE YOU LILY BASH, THE SMALLEST AND BRAVEST WOMAN EVER TO WALK ON WINGS!"

The audience stands and cheers as Ruthie's biplane passes over the racetrack. The small figure in the passenger cockpit is Miss Bash, dressed in a costume much like Ruthie's, including a leather helmet and goggles and a white silk scarf that ripples like a banner in the breeze. As they fly slowly by the grandstands, Lily casually steps out onto the lower wing, holding on with one hand so she can wave at those of us below. Making it look as easy and safe, as if she's stepped out of an automobile onto solid ground.

All that saves her from being swept from the wing is the grip of one small hand. As if that's not dangerous enough, she stands on tiptoe on the edge of the cockpit and from there crawls up onto the top wing, hanging on for dear life.

I have a bad feeling. A bad, bad feeling.

10. *Alone in This World*

THE GRANDSTANDS ARE suddenly quiet. No cheers, no chanting Lily's name, no calling for popcorn and soda. Respectful silence. Like we don't want to disturb the tiny, fearless woman. Let her find her balance on the upper wing. Let her not fall. Please, God, let her not fall!

Lily crawls to the center, where a thin pipe rises through the wing. It's hard to tell what she's doing, but she must somehow be attaching herself to the pipe. After a long minute she stands up, lifting her hands over her head in triumph. Look at me, the bravest woman in the world! Or quite possibly the most reckless, because at that moment Ruthie aims the Jenny almost straight up, starting one of her famous loop the loops.

At the top of the loop Lily is hanging upside down. Impossible! Why does she not fall? And then the Jenny is diving, coming out of the loop a hundred feet or so above the ground. Lily's short dark hair whips in the wind. As the biplane zooms past the grandstands we can see that she's laughing, as if she's just heard the funniest joke ever.

Laughing in the face of death. That must be what makes a daredevil a daredevil. Something I could never ever be.

"Popcorn! Hey, popcorn!"

———

When the last bag has been sold, I hurry out to where Ruthie's biplane has been parked not far from the tents. Wanting to see with my own eyes the secret of why the tiny stuntwoman did not fall. Turns out it's nothing fancy. Two sturdy leather straps, one for the ankles, one for the waist.

Later I'm told that Lily Bash does not own a parachute. The stunts take place at such a low altitude that a parachute would never have time to open. So, it's those two straps that keep her alive.

Brave, and also very dangerous, I decide.

I help Mrs. Mangano clean out the popcorn kettle and tidy up her cooking area so we can be ready for the next show. But when I try to share out some of the money I made with her help, she raises a hand like a traffic cop to stop me. "No, no! You keep! You keep!"

I know she's not mad or insulted because she messes my hair and tells me I'm a good boy. Part of me hates being treated like a little boy—I'm twelve!—and part of me loves it that such a nice lady has taken an interest. And think about it—I'm barely arrived at the flying circus, and already I made friends with the cook! By the end of the summer I'll be as round as a medicine ball. If you don't think that's a fine idea, you haven't been half starved for most of your life.

One thing I learn the hard way. Being the popcorn boy is no picnic. First, I make it and bag it, then trudge up and down the grandstands passing it out. Then run for the next batch and do it all over again. Ruthie was right—it gets so busy I don't have time to look up. Maybe that's good, because watching the stunts makes me worried about that look in Jo's eyes, the first time she saw a dare-devil in action.

A look that said, why not me?

11. *Dead Right, Almost*

I FALL ASLEEP worried about my sister and what the future holds for us. What happens when the flying season is over? Will Ruthie make sure we're "well situated," and what does that mean exactly?

Next thing I'm waking up from a nightmare that leaves my heart pounding.

In the dream, the tent had collapsed and I was trapped under it, unable to move, unable to breathe.

It's only a dream, I tell myself, but it takes awhile to calm down, and I never do fall back to sleep.

When I was four years old, my favorite game was *cache-cache*, hide-and-seek. Until it wasn't. This one time I decided to hide in the trunk where Mama kept linens, which happened to be in the bedroom. To make sure Jo couldn't find me, I pulled the lid shut.

It clicked.

I was trapped inside the linen trunk with no room to turn, no room to breathe, or so it seemed. Darkness squeezed from all sides. I remember the sheer terror that made me scream for help, but not the scream itself. Next thing, Jo is lifting the lid, taking me in her arms, soothing me as I bawled like a baby.

Never again would I enter small spaces, for any reason. I can't bear it, the thought of darkness squeezing the breath out of me.

———

That day is pack-up day, so it helps I was up early. The circus is moving to a new location more than fifty miles away. A hired crew, big strapping fellows from the French lumber camps, arrive to take down the tents, fold them a certain way, bundle up the tentpoles, and load everything onto a little parade of trucks. The trucks, piled so high with gear they look like they might tip over, take us to the train station in Waterville, where everything is transferred to railway flatcars.

Before sunrise, Jo and I were packing oil lamps and rugs into special crates. Pitching in with the regular crew and the hired men. Now we're waiting to board the train, each of us with a canvas duffel bag provided by Ruthie, and a brown bag breakfast courtesy of Mrs. Mangano, who always seems to be worried that somebody somewhere might be starving.

We open the paper bags and find fried egg sandwiches on toasted English muffins and small bottles of cold milk. We sit on a bench and enjoy the feast as the train is loaded.

"What a life we're living, Davy! I was only ever out of Biddeford once, and now the whole state is ours to explore."

That makes me laugh. "I've mostly been exploring the state of popcorn."

"You know what I mean, silly," she says, her eyes bright. "The world is our oyster."

"Never had an oyster. Have you?"

"Stop it! I'm saying our luck has changed. Can you at least agree with that?"

"Sorry, Jo. Just kidding. 'Course it has. If Ruthie hadn't taken us on for the summer, the nuns would have sent me to the boys' home for sure. They still might, once we're back in Biddeford."

"I'd never let that happen," Jo says.

"Might be you couldn't stop them," I say with a shrug. "We'll face that when the summer's over."

Jo gets one of her looks, the look that means she's disappointed in me. "Davy? We must put our faith in Ruthie. She will see us right. Whatever needs to be done, she will do."

I nod in agreement but can't help thinking, *What if what needs to be done is send me off to the so-called home for boys, which is a polite word for orphanage?*

"Trust in Ruthie, yes," Jo continues, nodding eagerly. "But I've been thinking Mama deserves some of the credit. She had the courage to write that letter. She was so low and sick, Davy, but she was looking out for us."

I agree with all my heart but don't want to talk about it just yet. Jo picks up on that and changes the subject. "Guess what? Ruthie promised to take me for a ride."

"In the Cadillac?"

Jo looks at me sideways. "You know better." With a smile, she points to the sky. "Don't worry. There's no danger in a flight over the fairgrounds. We won't be flying any loop the loops, or any stunts, period. It's just so I can feel what it's like to be in the air. Hey, don't look so worried!"

"I'm not worried," I lie. "Just be sure you stay in the cockpit."

"I promise!" she says with a laugh.

———

My mood improves when we board the train. The conductor takes us to Ruthie's private railway car—I never knew she had one!—and shows us to our upholstered seats.

"Jo, did you know about this?" I ask eagerly, bouncing on the seat.

"Not until this morning. Feels like we're really special. Like royalty or film stars."

Except for Mrs. Mangano, who is napping, we have the car almost to ourselves. Ruthie and Captain Merriman are piloting their biplanes to Lewiston. Tony Martini is driving the Bugatti over the road, and the tall man with the hat—his name is Patrice Boudreau—has taken charge of the Cadillac.

"The poor fellow has to wear a chauffer's uniform to drive the car," Jo says. "That's what Captain Merriman suggested, and Patrice agreed. Police see a Frenchman behind the wheel, they'll pull him over and ask for his papers. He has but a few words of English, so they'd likely arrest him. Possibly even deport him."

"I'd wear a uniform if it meant I could drive that car."

"That's not what I meant."

"I know. But I would."

"With the KKK rising, we all have to be extra careful. Hard to believe, but the newspapers say that some of the police march with them, and do their bidding."

It turns out she was right about the Klan.

Dead right, almost.

12. *In Which We Are Invaded*

THE NEXT DAY is Sunday, and with the first performance not until afternoon, Ruthie suggests that we take the opportunity to attend Mass in downtown Lewiston, not far from the fairgrounds. She drives her shiny red Cadillac over a bridge that spans a river, and suddenly we are in another city. Or so it seems to my startled eyes.

"*Le Petit Canada*," Ruthie explains. "Little Canada. When French Canadians immigrated to Maine to work the textile mills, they brought Quebec with them. Or as near as was possible. See how the streets curve? Across the river on the English side the streets are laid out like a grid, but here we like the curve because it reminds us of the old city of Quebec. We built our little markets and cafés, our churches and our own schools; we publish our own newspapers. We are poor because the mills pay so little, but we are rich in so many other ways."

The tone of her voice makes me pay attention. Normally Ruthie is upbeat and energetic, but as she describes her old neighborhood, she sounds almost sad. Sad, but somehow proud. "Much as I love this place, our city within a city, I wanted something more. I wanted to be out in the world having adventures, but that seemed impossible. Then a great-grandmother passed away in Canada—she had a popular bakery in the old city—and the dear sweet woman left me three thousand dollars to pay for an education." Ruthie pulls over on a narrow street and sets the handbrake. She turns to us and grins, her sadness forgotten. "I'm sure she had college in mind, but I used the inheritance to buy a flying machine from the Curtiss Company and enroll in flight school. Everything changed overnight."

"You're so brave," Jo says, her eyes huge.

Ruthie shrugs. "I saw my chance and took it. But I'll never forget where I came from."

We follow her for a few blocks, until a good-sized church comes into view. Brown brick, with arched stained-glass windows and a tall white steeple. The organ is playing as we enter and find seats in the last row. The church is full of worshippers reading from their missals or whispering quietly among themselves as they wait for Mass to begin.

"This is where I was baptized," Ruthie whispers. "As was your mother. We were in the church school together until her family moved to Biddeford."

Above us, the choir begins "Gloria." We rise and sing along to the familiar hymn in French.

An acolyte enters, swinging a metal incense burner, and the procession begins. Altar boys hold up the crucifix and the paired candles, and behind them an elderly priest in elegant robes holds the Book of the Gospels. The procession gets as far as the entrance to the altar when the wide front doors to the church are thrown violently open.

We are frozen in our pews, shocked by the thunderous banging of the wooden doors and by what happens next. A great clopping noise echoes throughout the church. The sound is vast and disturbing. The sound is impossible. We watch in astonishment as a large white horse clatters into the church, nostrils steaming. The great horse has white satin robes, as does the rider holding the reins.

White robes and a pointed white hood, with cutouts for his gleaming blue eyes.

"OUT!" the Klansman roars. "GET OUT OF OUR COUNTRY, YOU PAPIST DEVILS!"

13. *What Makes Him Hateful*

NEXT THING I know, Ruthie has us in her grip. She drags Jo and me up the side aisle toward the altar. Behind us, worshippers are choosing sides. Those who will shelter in the supposed safety of the holy church, and those who will drive the Klansman and his horse into the street. There is much shouting. Even, to my shocked ears, some lively cursing.

The altar boys grab ahold of the long, heavy candleholders, and advance down the center aisle, looking terrified and ferocious. "Glory be to God!" they shout in French, and charge into the fray.

"Over there!" Ruthie shouts above the tumult. "Through the vestry! There's an exit to the street!"

She drags us into a medium-sized room that smells of incense and cedar closets. Priest vestments hang from open cupboards. We're not supposed to be here, but Ruthie says God won't mind, not this once.

"Through that door, children. Quickly!"

Suddenly we're outside, in a narrow alley that leads to the street. Men are shouting. Horses are making fearful noises. Sirens wail in the distance.

"Keeps your backs to the wall and follow me!"

We follow her instructions and creep along the dark bricks, in the shadow of the church building. Ruthie's goal is to make it to her Cadillac and flee the danger that is rapidly unfolding. We peek around the corner and are astonished.

Worshippers who had been so quietly expecting to celebrate Mass have emptied out of the church in their suits and ties and hats. Raising fists to defend themselves and their place of worship. More men stream from the tenements to join them, wielding whatever weapons come to hand. Sticks, shovels. Women, too, with rolling pins, mops, and brooms. The French people of Little Canada. Franco Americans, as we call ourselves. Everybody trying to shout down the head Klansman, still astride his horse although retreated to the street in front of the church steps. He's accompanied by many other Klansmen, fifty or more, some of them wearing hoods and others bareheaded, as if proud to make themselves known. Several brandish burning torches, and a white wooden cross has been set afire and placed on the church steps.

The man on the magnificent white horse bellows loud enough to be heard above the roar, "We will not be overrun by the lower races! Not by Blacks! Not by foreigners of such low birth they might as well be worms! Frenchmen! Frog-eating Frenchmen! Garlic-stinking Italians! Dirty Irish! Filthy Jews! Catholics! Papists! Creatures of Rome! Go back where you came from, you scum, you vermin! This nation, this white Anglo-Saxon nation, refuses to be replaced by filthy immigrants! Get out! Get out! If you want to live, get out!"

"Pay him no heed!" Ruthie says earnestly. "Fear has made him hateful."

"What's a Papist?" I want to know. "Is he talking about the Pope?"

"Never mind. We have no time for this. Move, children, move!"

Ruthie is trying to shepherd us around the corner to where the car is parked, but when we finally get there, the street has been blocked by half a dozen Lewiston police cars. Uniformed officers idle in the street, arms folded, or hands on their billy clubs.

Their captain, a large and imposing man with a chin

like the prow of a ship, marches over and confronts Ruthie. "I know you. The lady flier. What are you doing here?"

"Going to church," Ruthie says, an edge to her voice. "What are *you* doing here? Why aren't you chasing those horrible men away? Why aren't you arresting them?"

He gives her a long, hard look. "First Amendment. Constitution guarantees free speech and assembly. Like it or not, the Klan has a right to march. They're on the march all over the state."

Sounds like he's proud to hear it. Ruthie immediately drops her accusatory tone and begs that the police cars be moved so she can get the children to safety. Grudgingly, they do so, and moments later we're on our way.

Jo says bitterly, "That cop should be wearing his hood and robe."

Ruthie checks her rearview mirrors, making sure we've not been followed. "You picked up on that, did you? Not surprising, really. The Klan has more than a hundred thousand recruits in Maine. That's one out of seven residents, including women and children. It stands to reason that their ranks include some police officers."

Back at the fairgrounds, Ruthie quietly confers with Captain Merriman. He nods and marches off, as if on a mission.

"We've decided to post lookouts," she says. "Just to be safe."

———

Later we see in the papers that the Klan was driven out of Little Canada and nearly overwhelmed as they retreated across the bridge. The police finally had to intervene to protect the men in the pointy hoods, who continued their march through the city of Lewiston, urging residents to rise up against the "foreign invaders."

They're talking about me and Jo.

14. *A Head Full of Money*

THAT EVENING, AFTER the last show, I beg Ruthie to let me watch the men play cards in their tent.

"Watch?" she says, eyeing me with great care. "Just observe, not join in?"

"No, ma'am."

"Wait here."

Ruthie marches to the big tent, slips inside. I hear her murmuring, deep voices responding, and then laughter. She emerges and, with a slight bow and sweep of her arm, encourages me to enter. She strides away with a cheerful "Have fun, young man!"

Inside, the air is ripe with cigar smoke. Three men, seated at a card table under an oil lamp, wave at me in a friendly way. Tony Martini, the daredevil and race car driver; Patrice Boudreau, the hat man; and Ronan

O'Ryan, the ace mechanic who keeps everything running.

"Hello, Davy. Come join us!" roars O'Ryan, with an Irish lilt to his voice. "The boss made us promise not to take a penny offa you. As if we'd cheat a boy!"

The way the men grin makes me glad that Ruthie extracted her promise.

"Heard you and your sister was in the middle of the troubles this morning," Ronan says. "Is it true those fools rode a horse into the church?"

I nod.

He shakes his head and takes a thoughtful puff on his cigar. "'Tis a great mystery, why they hate them that took the jobs they didn't want. A farmhand in Rumford lives the life of a king compared to them that works the textile mills. So why begrudge the poor immigrant, eh? Makes no sense. It's like wasps have gotten into their brains and stung 'em with mad venom."

Patrice the hat man asks me a question in French. He has to repeat it because my French isn't very good. Mama believed that if we were ever to escape life in the mills, we must be English speakers. But eventually I'm able to understand that Patrice wants to know if the priests fought the Klansmen. I tell him I don't know about the priests, but the altar boys were in the crowd that drove them away.

He claps a friendly hand on my shoulder. *"Bien. Je comprends."*

Good. I understand.

Tony Martini fans a deck of cards. "Pick one," he suggests. "Put in pocket."

I pick a card and slip it into my shirt pocket. He shuffles the cards and sets them aside. He frowns and shakes his head, then reaches out and plucks a coin from my ear. Before I can react, he plucks two more coins from my nose. He chuckles, his eyes lighting up with merriment, and gives me the coins.

O'Ryan says, "You've a head full of money, or so it seems. Clever man, Signor Bellini."

The mechanic explains that Tony Martini is a stage name. Antonio Giuseppe Bellini was once a trapeze artist in a family circus, famous throughout Europe. He also has skills as a close-up magician, as he has just demonstrated. Signor Bellini speaks only a little English, but somehow makes himself understood by expression and gesture.

The Italian daredevil nods eagerly and makes a face. He touches his throat and looks puzzled. He coughs and then seems to retrieve a playing card from inside his mouth. He holds it up. It's my card! I check my empty pocket and realize he must have distracted me when he was pulling coins out of my ears.

"That's amazing."

Bellini makes a little bow and says, *"Grazie."*

I don't need a translator to know that means thanks. Fact is, me and Jo grew up hearing lots of languages in the Biddeford tenements. French, English, Italian, Polish, Yiddish—those I recognize when I hear them, even if I don't know what the words mean. Three languages being spoken at this little card table, but nobody seems to mind. Mostly because they're not playing cards so much as letting themselves be entertained by Bellini's astonishing skills. He pulls cards out of pockets, from behind the head, out of thin air. He makes the cards dance as he shuffles. He looks like he's having so much fun that it makes everybody happy to be in his company.

When the three men head off to bed—they have to be well rested for tomorrow's air show—I slip away to my own cot and fall asleep as soon as my head hits the pillow.

In my dream, I'm a little boy and Papa pretends to pull coins from my nose. I'm so happy I don't want the dream to end, but it does when Jo leans through the curtain. "Hey, Davy!" she calls out. "Time to rise and shine. Maggie's cooking baked eggs and sausage, Italian style."

I don't know what that is, exactly, but I can't wait to find out.

15. Say Hello to the Ants

THE BEST THING about being crew on Ruthie Reynard's Flying Circus is not the airplanes or the stunts, great as they are: It's the breakfast. Back home, in the darkest days of Mama's illness, we were lucky to share a small bowl of oatmeal. On holy days that didn't require fasting, we got a boiled egg, and were glad of it. So, Mrs. Mangano's all-you-can-eat-and-then-one-bite-more breakfast is a gift from heaven, for which I say a prayer of thanks, head bowed, before stuffing myself on crispy ham dishes, and garlic potatoes, and baked eggs, and fluffy scrambled eggs, and buttery cinnamon toast dazzled with powdered sugar. Plus, perfectly ripened pears and wild blueberries!

Jo advises me to slow down, or risk having my stomach blow out like a bad tire.

"The food is wonderful, but you don't have to eat all of it."

I groan, holding my belly. "I don't want to insult the cook."

Jo laughs. "Remember, gluttony is a sin."

"That can't be right," I protest. "Hunger should be a sin, not eating your fill."

"There's bicarbonate soda in the tent if you need it." She rises from the table, off to meet Ruthie to learn about keeping the books. My big sister is eager to please, and why not? This is the opportunity of a lifetime.

I'm about to go to work in Maggie's kitchen when stuntman Tony Martini taps me on the shoulder and asks how tall I am.

"You mean how short," I respond, none too happily.

Try being the shortest boy in class and see how you like being constantly reminded of your size. Hey, short stuff. Say hello to the ants, pipsqueak. Sorry, I didn't see you down there. Hey, Tiny, do you stand on a box to brush your teeth?

Very funny. Hilarious.

"Okay," he says, holding out the flat of his hand, as if to measure the distance between the top of my head and the ground. "How short?"

His expression is serious, and I get the sense that he's

not making fun of me. For some reason my height, or lack of it, is important information.

I shrug and tell him. He nods thoughtfully. "I go train station, pick up new race car, bring here. Okay?"

"Sure, okay." New race car, that's interesting, but what does it have to do with me?

"How you say, something in my brain? Idea! Big fun! You wait?"

From the canteen tent I can scrub out the popcorn kettle and still keep an eye on the racetrack, alert for the arrival of any new vehicles. Why does Tony want to know my height? The famous stuntman wasn't trying to be mean or cruel, of that I am sure. And what does he mean by "big fun"?

Grown-ups can be so mysterious.

16. *Impossible*

AN HOUR OR so later, a cloud of dust rises over the tree-tops. The sure sign of an approaching vehicle. I run out to catch a glimpse of the new car. When it comes skidding around the corner, spitting gravel and dirt, I expect to see Tony behind the wheel. The car zooms onto the track, giving me a clear view, and I'm stunned by the fact that Tony isn't driving.

No one is. The shiny blue Alfa Romeo P2 Grand Prix race car has two seats, and both are empty.

Impossible. It's as likely a pig sprouts wings as a race car drives itself. And yet there it is, careening around the track at high speed, engine roaring on eight supercharged cylinders. My first thought is the gas pedal got stuck and Tony fell out of the car. But no, the blue beast is not out of control. Somehow it is being expertly steered. It changes gears smoothly and drifts through the turns as if being driven by a professional driver.

How can this be? The answer is, it can't. And yet there it is, in plain view.

Circus crew pour out of the tents to cheer on the impossible. Someone laughs and calls it a "ghost car."

Mrs. Mangano stoutly disagrees. "Is no ghost. Is stunt! Big stunt!"

Maggie is proved right when the Alfa Romeo finally slows down and veers carefully off the track. It comes to a stop. The engine shuts down. I race to the vehicle, peering into the cockpit.

Empty.

Then, to my amazement, a hand appears between the two seats. A hand that waves hello.

"Ciao, amici!"

Tony's voice coming from behind the seats, where he has been hidden away, operating a small steering wheel and a hand throttle.

"Big fun!" he says, crawling out from his hiding spot. He shakes my hand enthusiastically and points back at the car. *"Tutto tuo. Devi guidare!"*

I've no idea what that means until Mrs. Mangano provides a helpful translation. "He say, the car is yours, and you must drive it."

17. *The Donkey Is Me*

My FIRST THOUGHT is that my feet won't reach the pedals. Then Maggie explains that Tony wants me to look like I'm driving when in fact he will be steering from behind the seats. Me "driving" is part of the act.

"I don't get it," I say. "Is it supposed to be funny?"

As Maggie explains, Tony's eyes light up. He speaks rapidly, waving his hands.

"Tony say he forget most important part. The costume!"

As if to demonstrate, he retrieves a leather duffel bag from the floor of the cockpit, snaps it open, and displays a costume. *"Comprendere?"* he asks in a confidential tone. "Understand?"

What I see makes me grin so hard my face hurts. Fantastic! I can't wait to try it on.

"Tony remember this act at circus in Rome," Maggie explains. "He say audience love."

He may be right, but we'll just have to see if the audience in Waterville, Maine, agrees with Rome.

———

The deal is, I remain in the stands selling popcorn until ten minutes before showtime. We share the details of the stunt with Ruthie, who instantly approves. "It just might work," she says. "Give it your best shot."

At the agreed-upon time I slip away, as if to fetch more popcorn. The new car has been parked under one of the grandstands, concealed by a canvas panel. Tony is already secretly in place behind the seats. I slip into the costume, adjust the bulky headpiece, and take my place in the driver's seat, crouching on the seat, hands—actually, hoofs—on the wheel.

High above us, our announcer welcomes the crowd.

"GOOD AFTERNOON, LADIES AND GENTS AND CHILDREN OF ALL AGES. WELCOME TO THE RUTHIE REYNARD FLYING CIRCUS, AND PREPARE TO BE AMAZED! THIS IS YOUR LUCKY DAY, FOR A BRAND-NEW RACING MACHINE HAS JUST JOINED OUR TEAM. AN ALFA ROMEO P2 GRAND PRIX,

CAPABLE OF ACHIEVING ONE HUNDRED AND FIFTY MILES PER HOUR! BUT THE MOST AMAZING THING ISN'T THE SPEED, IT IS THE ADVANCED ENGINEERING. THIS CAR IS SO EASY TO DRIVE, A DONKEY COULD DO IT! AND IF YOU DON'T BELIEVE ME, BELIEVE YOUR EYES!"

Tony starts the engine and we roar out from under the stands. As you probably guessed, the donkey is me. I wiggle around in the costume, waving my big, padded donkey hoofs and honking the horn. Toot! Toot! Toot! The crowd roars its approval.

They love it when, later, I roll on my back in the dirt like a real donkey. The more I act the part of a cartoonish creature, the more they laugh and cheer. Every eye in the grandstands is focused on me, and that feels both strange and wonderful. They can't see my real face, but I'm the star of the show. Me, little Davy Michaud, small enough to fit in the child-sized costume. For the first time in my life I'm exactly the right size.

We speed around the track for one lap, showing off the Alfa Romeo's power. The car screeches to a halt in front of the grandstands. I leap out, remove the headpiece, and take a bow.

"Donkey Boy! Donkey Boy!"

The announcer shouts louder than the raucous

crowd. "LADIES AND GENTS, PUT YOUR HANDS TOGETHER FOR DAVID MICHAUD, THE YOUNGEST MEMBER OF OUR TEAM! IT'S HOT INSIDE THAT COSTUME, BUT FOR DAVY THE PERFORMANCE WAS 'NO SWEAT.'"

"Donkey Boy! Donkey Boy!"

Jo waves from the front row, looking as pleased for me as I've ever seen her. I wave back, taking another bow, and that's the cue for Tony to finish the act. As I'm bowing and hamming it up, the driverless car suddenly backs away from me and then jerks to a stop, as if waiting for me to respond. I pretend to be surprised and chase after it. The car backs away just as my "hoof" touches the hood.

We keep this up for two times more—the futile chase, the driverless car backing away—and then the Alfa Romeo spins around and roars off in a cloud of dust.

The crowd goes nuts. Sorry, but there's no other way to explain it. They came to the fairgrounds expecting airplanes, not a famous circus act adapted for our show, but they absolutely adore the antics of the little donkey boy.

Best part, they recognize me as the kid hawking popcorn, and once I'm back in the stands, I sell twice as much as usual. I'm going to be rich!

18. *Jo's Promise*

JO SEEKS ME out after the last air show and gives me a ferocious hug. "Little brother, you surprise me. You stole the show!"

"It's the donkey costume," I say, trying to sound modest. "That, and the driverless car."

She takes both of my hands in hers, looking me in the eyes, very serious. "No, it was you. Playing for laughs like a real professional. The audience *loved* you, Davy. They fear for the pilots and the daredevils, and root for their survival, most of them, but you they loved."

"Aw, shucks," I say, rolling my eyes.

"Stop it. I'm so happy for you, Davy. Mama and Papa would be, too."

I don't know what to say. It makes me happy and sad at the same time, which sounds impossible, but isn't.

There's no sign of the Klan for the next few days. As I work the stands, selling popcorn, and on the racetrack in costume, hamming it up for cheering crowds, my concern about the men in white robes fades away. Besides, there's another thing that takes all my attention.

My sister, Jo, waving from the front cockpit of Ruthie's Jenny. She's dressed in a borrowed leather helmet and goggles and rippling scarf, just like the wing walker Lily Bash, who Jo so admires. The Jenny circles the fairgrounds before the opening show, gently banking through the turns. As Jo promised, there are no stunt moves. No loop the loops, no flying upside down.

When the ride is over, Ruthie lands her flying machine on the racetrack, smooth as can be. Jo leaps out of the front cockpit.

"Davy! It was wonderful! Ruthie says you can have a ride anytime you want. You'll see how safe it feels."

"Thanks, I'll take my chances on the ground. Ninety miles an hour in a Grand Prix race car is thrill enough for me. So, does this mean you want to be a pilot?"

"I don't know. Maybe."

"Promise me you'll be careful."

I see a hug coming my way and manage to dodge it.

Jo catches my hand, turns me around. "Davy? Don't worry, I won't take any chances."

"Promise?"

"I promise."

Jo's promise means a lot, but not enough to keep me from being concerned.

19. *Her Broom Sweeps Clean*

WE'VE BEEN KEEPING an eye out for the men in the
pointy hoods, but it turns out Klansmen don't always
appear in costume. When the gates open at our next venue,
the Union Fair, a ruddy-faced man in a suit and hat
strides through, carrying a small crate. He's a proper-
looking fellow, with a buttoned waistcoat and a sizable fob
hanging from his watch pocket. Could be a banker, maybe,
or a well-dressed salesman.

What he's selling takes me by surprise. I happen to be
in the vicinity, preparing the first batch of popcorn and
looking forward to another turn around the track as the
now-famous Donkey Boy. Not really paying close attention
to the banker type until he places the crate on the ground
near the grandstands. He then steps atop the crate to give a
speech.

"My fellow white Americans! We are in danger! The lower races seek to overwhelm us! To replace us! It is happening right here in the great state of Maine! We have been overrun by ignorant immigrants and filthy foreigners! If we fail to drive them out, our white race will be destroyed!"

As he harangues the passing crowd, two big, burly men stand by, handing out pamphlets. They could be farmers or prison guards—strong, tough men for sure.

"Those of you in the ruling race, if you want to know the truth, read this pamphlet! Justice for the white race is all we ask! Read about the cunning conspiracy that seeks to overwhelm us with foreigners! Jews! Italians! Irish! French! The filthy and the wicked, in league to replace us! I say banish them! Drive them from this land!"

Most of the customers toss the pamphlet to the ground, unread, but others carefully fold it and place it in their pockets. Too many others, in my opinion. What are they thinking?

"You stop! *Smettere di mentire!* Stop lying! *Noi amiamo l'America!* We love America!"

That's Maggie Mangano in her kitchen apron, hands on her hips, calling out his lies. Eyes blazing, she lets him have it.

"We build your railroads! Your factories! Your schools!

With our hands, our backs, our hearts! We come in peace to work, to live, to be American! *Come osi*, how dare you!"

The two bruisers confer with their boss and quickly advance on Maggie with their fists raised. She stands her ground, cursing at them in Italian, something about them being cowards.

I race to her side, wishing I were twice as tall. "Leave her alone, you rotten bullies!"

If I had any sense I'd run for it. Instead I raise my own puny fists. The bruisers laugh and scuff their feet like bulls about to charge.

They're almost upon us when suddenly they stop in their tracks.

"That's right! Run, you bloody devils! Run back to your mamas! Get on with you!"

The Irishman Ronan O'Ryan, waving a broom like a weapon, is leading a charge of the circus family. Tony Martini, Patrice Boudreau, a couple of French lumberjacks hired to maintain the tents, all of them advancing like a small, determined army.

The bruisers and their loudmouthed friend turn tail and run, leaving their crate behind.

Ronan hands the broom to an astonished and grateful Maggie. "Sure, and I borrowed this without asking." He gestures in the direction of the departed hate-mongers, his

Irish lilt strong and true. "They say a new broom sweeps clean, but the likes of them leaves a certain stench behind. What do you say to that, me boyos?"

"The show must go on," Tony responds, grinning. He nudges my shoulder. "We make fun stunt, Davy, we make much laughter, help forget the bad men."

Trouble is, I can't forget.

20. *Marbles Will Not Do*

THE NEXT "GROUND day"—no shows scheduled—
happens to be Jo's birthday. Her eighteenth birthday. My
sister hasn't mentioned it to anyone, but I let the news slip
to my friend Mrs. Mangano, and next thing you know she's
throwing a party and everyone's invited for later that afternoon. That gives Maggie time to bake a cake and decorate
the canteen.

I help her string paper flower blossoms around the
entrance to the tent, and put glasses of real cut flowers on
the tables. She keeps clapping her hands together and singing the Italian version of "Happy Birthday" to herself.
Beaming like it was her own birthday, not Jo's.

I don't remember my grandmothers, who died young,
like so many in the mills, but I hope they were like Mrs.
Mangano, who has been so kind to me and Jo.

Ruthie strides in and takes me aside. "Come with me," she says, and leads me to the women's tent. When she's sure there's no one else around, especially Jo, she asks, "Davy, do you have a birthday present in mind for your sister?"

I nod. "Marbles. A big bag of marbles from the five and dime. Really good ones!"

Ruthie chuckles and shakes her head. "Your sister becomes an adult today. I think we can do better than a bag of marbles."

"But Jo loves to play marbles! She's really good."

"That's as may be, but marbles will not do. I have another idea, but only if you approve."

She opens a steamer trunk, pulls out a storage tray, and shows me what she has in mind.

"Wow! It's really perfect, and Jo will love it. But it's your idea; shouldn't you be the one to give it to her?"

Ruthie smiles in a kindly fashion. "It will mean so much more coming from you. As far as your sister is concerned, yours is the only opinion that truly matters."

———

Jo's cheeks turn pink when she realizes what me and Mrs. Mangano have been up to. "There's no need," she says. "I didn't want to make a fuss."

"Fuss?" Mrs. Mangano throws up her hands. "*Il tuo compleanno.* Your birthday. Good fuss! Fun fuss! Happy fuss!"

The rest of the flying circus crew begin to arrive. Lily Bash and Ronan O'Ryan carry in a windup Victrola and a stack of big band records. Soon they're doing the new dance craze called the Charleston. I've seen it in the newsreels, but never in person, and they make it look even more fun. Then Jo joins in and I about fall to the floor. How does my sister know how to do that crazy dance, kicking her legs sideways and tapping her heels with her hands? Where did she learn, or are girls just born knowing how?

After the Victrola winds down, Mrs. Mangano appears with a huge cake, candles blazing. We sing "Happy birthday, dear Josephine" in about three different languages. I have to say, Jo is beaming, beaming, beaming. Then she's crying and everybody is hugging her and Ruthie raises a glass of milk for a toast to the birthday girl—excuse me, woman—and says something about tragedy and joy living side by side, and how we must seize the day and live life to its fullest. Then it's time for cards and presents. Jo gets some beautiful, flowery cards and a bottle of real French perfume from Ruthie.

My present is on-purpose last. Jo unwraps it and opens

the lid of what looks like a thin shoebox. She takes out my gift to her, as recommended by Ruthie: a brand-new leather flying helmet and matching goggles.

Jo's eyes find me. Her whole face lights up. "Davy, come here!" and she throws a hug on me that nearly breaks my spine.

I don't have to say it because the gift spoke for me, as Ruthie knew it would. It means I'm okay with her flying. Yes, I will continue to worry, but I'll be rooting for her all the way, and doing my best to share her sense of joy at being in the air, free as a bird. Free as a poor French girl who has escaped the Biddeford mills, and is determined to have a life that doesn't involve inhaling cotton dust.

Happy birthday, big sister!

———

Why would such a happy day end with a nightmare? In the dream it is night, a night as dark as sleep. I'm running barefoot along the Saco River bank, fleeing from the nuns. They call my name, which echoes off the mill buildings and fills me with dread.

Davy Michaud! God loves you!

Maybe, but the nuns want to send me away. They

call it a school for boys, because orphanage sounds so bleak.

I run until I wake up, and am careful to hide my tears.

Ruthie Reynard is a good and kind person. She'd never let the dream come true. Would she?

21. *The Fastest Female Alive*

IT BEGINS AS a growl on the wind. Five o'clock on a summer evening, and still loads of daylight. Our circus crew gathers at the racetrack, awaiting the arrival of a new aviator. New to the show, I should say, not to the skill of flying.

The growl becomes a roar, and then an explosion of wind as a bright red biplane zooms low at impossible speed. Nothing can move that fast, can it?

"Curtiss R-6!" Ruthie shouts. "V-12 engine! Two hundred miles an hour! Maybe more!"

The powerful flying machine banks smoothly and returns for another speed run over the racetrack. A blur of cherry red, but I catch a glimpse of the name on the fuselage: *Liberty Belle*. After another astonishing pass, the biplane lands on the grass and rolls to a stop. Even standing still it looks sleek and fast. The single cockpit sits behind one of the most powerful aircraft engines in the world.

Out of the cockpit slips a tall, slender woman with raven-black hair, large brown eyes, and a shy smile. Miss Elsie Belinski, stage name Elsie Bell. An old friend of Ruthie's, from the days of flying school. "Elsie, you devil, I am so jealous! Our Jennys top out at seventy miles an hour."

"Nothing wrong with a Jenny," Elsie responds. "It has served you well. You still hold the record on loop the loops, last I heard."

"Correct," says Ruthie with a grin.

"One of these days we'll have to see about that," Elsie teases. "I'm famished; what's for supper?"

———

Miss Belinski has nothing but compliments for Maggie's cooking, but I notice she doesn't eat much. Pushes the food around in the same way that Ruthie sometimes does on flying days.

Nerves, I suppose, although she does not show it. Elsie is not so well known as Ruthie, but hopes to change that.

"I first saw Ruthie perform at an air show in Lynn, Massachusetts, and from that day I wanted to learn to fly.

Truth is, I wanted to *be* her, flying so free and unafraid."

Jo is nodding in agreement, and it becomes clear that our famous cousin has the power to inspire young women to join the small sisterhood of female pilots. It is a power she carries lightly, rolling her eyes at Elsie's words.

"Oh, stop," Ruthie says, waving away the compliments. "You were born to fly, Elsie, and would have done so regardless."

"Whatever you say," Elsie responds with a laugh. "The truth is, before that fateful air show I wanted to drive race cars. So there!"

The talk turns to aircraft, as it always seems to do with aviators. The subject is *Liberty Belle*, the Curtiss R-6, identical to the model that holds the world speed record of two hundred and forty miles per hour.

"That was average speed over a five-mile course around pylons," Elsie explains. "On a straight shot, flat out, *Belle* can hit two fifty."

"No!"

Captain Merriman, who has been listening attentively, leans forward, placing his hands upon the table. "Remarkable," he says. "I suggest you be billed as 'The Fastest Female Alive,' and close each show with a demonstration run."

Ruthie instantly agrees.

22. *What Stops Me in My Tracks*

THINGS START TO unravel when we arrive at the Skowhegan Fairgrounds. The day starts out perfect, thanks to Mrs. Mangano's fabulous breakfast. Heaping plates of Italian sausage, three kinds of baked eggs, a tomato and cheese casserole, and spicy sliced potatoes that smell so delicious I'm ready to snap the aroma out of the air like a dog. Also, Maggie's version of French toast: instead of regular bread, she uses slices of an Italian bread called panettone. Real maple syrup and plenty of butter, of course. Yum!

Jo, sitting across the table from me, looks up from her plate and says, "David Michaud, I swear you have grown an inch and put some meat on your skinny bones."

The thing is, until we joined the flying circus, I never realized that I was hungry all the time. Mama kept us from starving after Papa died, but just barely. I don't mention that Jo has put some meat on her own bones, and that it looks good on her. Looks healthy, like the color in her cheeks.

"Do you have plans for the morning?" Jo wants to know.

"We report to work at two p.m., right? I was thinking, until then I might visit the animals."

Skowhegan is one of the biggest agricultural fairs in the state, and that means loads of farm animals, from newborn chicks to draft horses. Being a mill town boy, I'm eager for the sight of livestock. Horses especially.

"Mind if I join you?" Jo asks.

"'Course not!"

A pleasant surprise, that my big sister would choose to spend time with me over airplanes. We stroll through the midway, not tempted by any of the fried foods, although the fresh doughnuts sure smell good. Jo steers us away from a fortune-teller and the man who guesses weights.

"The fortune-teller makes a fortune telling people what they want to hear, and the guess-your-weight man isn't guessing, he's had years of experience estimating size. He never loses. So, we keep our money, Davy, agreed?"

I've seen enough grifters working the fairs to know

she's right. After a quick saunter through the midway, where we watch an ax-throwing contest, draft horses dragging sleds loaded with stone, and kids chasing slippery piglets in the mud, we come to the biggest part of the fair. The agricultural exhibitions. Fine Morgan horses, sheep soft as pillows, their wool washed and shampooed to impress the judges. Hogs so big they might as well be steers. Prize dairy cows, Holstein, Guernsey, and Jersey. There are cattle of every breed, including a Texas longhorn, who's about as far from home as he can get and still be in the United States of America.

My favorite is Big Boy, a best-in-state Hereford bull. Big Boy is massive, near two thousand pounds of muscle and bone. They say Hereford bulls are well behaved, compared with some other breeds, but Big Boy has a look in his eyes that says he's the exception. He's in a small stall so he can't get running room, but he stomps his massive hoofs and snorts pure steam, marking his territory. The boy tending the stall warns us to keep back. Says Big Boy broke somebody's hand trying to pet him.

"He ain't no pet," the stall boy warns. "Look and learn, but don't touch."

I'm not tempted. Jo, wrinkling her nose, mentions that Big Boy has a peculiar perfume. "Smells like a barn full of sick cows" is how she puts it.

"You want to get in that stall and clean up behind him?" I ask, and Jo giggles and shakes her head.

As we head back to the airfield, I have no idea what a big smelly deal Big Boy will be to the flying circus.

———

I make the popcorn, fill the carrier with the buttery paper bags, and patrol the grandstands as they gradually fill up with spectators eager to see the air show. Farmers and their families, merchants, shopkeepers, and office workers, as well as those few mill workers who can afford the price of admission. The farm folks are boisterous, the mill workers eager but quiet, like they don't want to stir up a fuss. Typical audience, and it's looking to be a beautiful afternoon, with a fair breeze and clear skies.

I sell out the first batch of popcorn and am about to head down under the grandstands to don my costume when something stops me in my tracks.

BOOM! BOOM! BOOM!

BOOM! BOOM! BOOM!

A big bass drum, sounding cadence for a marching band. That's my first impression.

I couldn't have been more wrong.

23. *They Put Their Hands Together*

BOOM! BOOM! BOOM!

Louder, coming closer.

BOOM! BOOM! BOOM!

Everyone in the stands is craning to the right, straining to see what is making the commotion.

Closer. Closer. Close enough that we soon hear chanting voices responding to the big bass drum.

BOOM! BOOM! BOOM!

"K! K! K!"

BOOM! BOOM! BOOM!

"K! K! K!"

A collective gasp from the grandstands as Klansmen flood onto the parade grounds. KKK, as they've been chanting, announcing themselves. Hundreds of them in their gleaming white satin robes and their white hoods with eyeholes. An anonymous disguise meant to frighten—and it does, at least as far as I'm concerned. The Klansmen are not bothering with torches in the bright of the afternoon but instead are clutching baseball bats and staves, and a few with pitchforks held aloft.

At the head of the army rides their Grand Dragon, or Kleagle, or whatever he is, astride his great white charger. To my eyes, it is the same man who rode his horse into the French church in Lewiston. Same horse, same gleaming white hood and robe, same erect posture. Behind the horse is the drummer, boom-boom-boom, a tall, broad-shouldered fellow in a white robe and hood, banging on the biggest drum I've ever seen. A drum emblazoned with the letters *KKK*.

No hiding in the dark for these men. They march in full pride, showing off their costumes as they strut behind their leader. Avoiding horse droppings is a small inconvenience, compared with their fearless Anglo-Saxon heritage. I asked Jo what "Anglo-Saxon" means, exactly, and she explained it was supposed to refer to ancient German tribes who once dominated Northern Europe and the British Isles. But to the KKK it means their ancestors came from Northern Europe. Meaning English, German, and Scots, somehow, but not Irish, and certainly not French or

Italian or Spanish, who are, to the Klan, not really members of the white race because their blood has somehow been tainted.

Doesn't make sense, but there it is.

The army of white hoods takes formation behind their leader, who stops in the center of the fairgrounds, a few yards from the crowded grandstand. Two of the men hold the massive white horse by the bridle while their leader dismounts. With the hood highly peaked he looks about eight feet tall. Which I suppose is the idea. He wants us to think he's a giant among men.

He strides to the first row of the grandstand, surveying the crowd. Then, in a dramatic move, he slips off the hood and reveals his face. He has a massive head with close-cropped blond hair. His small, glittering eyes are the palest blue, staring over a prominent nose, long and thin. Adjusting his gold-trimmed robe, he steps into the grandstand as if he's a god, and we the peasants who worship him.

Up he comes, step by step, grand and regal.

As he marches higher, something happens that shocks me to my soul. Many of the farmers and merchants stand up and take off their hats, as if to show respect. A few even offer the Klan's famous salute, with their left hands splayed across their hearts and their right arms straight out from the shoulder. Their eyes glow with something that sends a cold bolt of fear down the length of my spine.

And then they put their hands together and applaud the Klan leader as he passes.

24. *The Eyes of the Klansmen Are upon Me*

OKAY, THE FACT that some of the people in the stands—
many of them—are applauding the Klan does more than
shock me to my soul. These are folks who've been buying
popcorn from me, giving me penny tips, cheering me on as
Donkey Boy. But the truth, the truth that opens like a
grave under my feet, is that in their hearts they despise me.
How else could they applaud those who make no secret of
hating me and my family and all those who have immigrated to work in the mills and factories?

The Grand-whatever-he-is ascends the grandstand like
a king ascending his throne. He seems to be coming for me
personally—the focused stare of his pale blue eyes—but he
passes me by without heed. His followers spread out behind
him like a stream of rippling white satin. Men in flowing
ropes and high-peaked hoods, waving their sticks and bats

and pitchforks, chanting "K! K! K!" to the beat of that enormous drum.

I step back from the edge of the stairway and find myself balancing on the plank seating. A Klansman spots me wobbling and waves the tines of his pitchfork under my chin.

He hisses, "Froggy froggy do! Get out of my country, French boy! Run for your life!"

I want to scream that it is my country, too, that I was born in Biddeford, Maine, but I'm too frightened of that pitchfork to respond. He cackles a laugh, triumphant over a small boy, and shakes his pitchfork. "White Anglo-Saxon Nation! White Anglo-Saxon Nation! White Anglo-Saxon Nation!"

His cry is taken up by his robed brothers, and by many in the crowd. I had assumed they paid to see the air show, but now I wonder if some of them were part of the invasion. They don't care about the flying circus. They're here to cheer on the Klan.

"WHITE ANGLO-SAXON NATION! WHITE ANGLO-SAXON NATION! WHITE ANGLO-SAXON NATION!"

Their leader, gathering the hem of his robe, launches himself up the steps. The show announcer, seeing the tide of white hoods, abandons his giant megaphone and flees.

Can't say I blame him. I'd leave if my way wasn't blocked by sneering, shouting Klansmen.

"WHITE NATION! WHITE NATION!"

The chant stops when their leader raises his fist. He holds it there, savoring the moment before he takes a deep breath.

"Hear the truth!" he roars into the megaphone. "This great nation, founded by proud members of the ruling Anglo-Saxon race, the purest of the human races, is being overrun by barely human scum! The Negro, the French, Italians, Irish, the Jew, all subhuman! All controlled by an international conspiracy of Jews in league with the Pope in Rome. They fiendishly plot to replace our white purity with filthy foreigners! Creatures who are lower than worms! Creatures who must be driven from our shores if the white race is to survive! If America as we know and love it is to survive! In the name of justice, join our cause! K! K! K! Ku Klux Klan!"

The crowd roars back, "K! K! K! KU KLUX KLAN!"

Every word of hatred hits me like a fist to the belly. More than anything, I want to flee with my hands over my ears. I dare not because the eyes of Klansmen are upon me, daring me to make a move.

Something grabs me by the ankle, nearly stopping my heart. Whatever it is won't let go. I sink to the bench, still holding my popcorn carrier, and try to shake loose.

The grip tightens on my ankle. "Davy! Davy Michaud! Look down!"

Below me, in the shadows under the stands, Ruthie grins up at me.

"What are you waiting for?" she wants to know.

25. *It's My Country, Too*

RUTHIE ENCOURAGES ME to abandon the popcorn carrier and slip down between the seats. She catches my dangling legs and lowers me to the ground.

"I didn't want to leave you behind. Tony has taken the Alfa Romeo to the train station. We're about to evacuate. Your sister is waiting."

We are not alone in the shadows under the grandstand. Many of the immigrant laborers are also slipping away, fearing to face the wrath of the bat-wielding Klansmen. We stood up to them in Lewiston when they invaded our church, but here we are outnumbered and out-armed.

Retreat is the only option. Or is it?

"Where is everybody?" I ask, meaning the rest of our circus crew.

"Guarding the biplanes," Ruthie says. "One man with

a pitchfork could tear a Jenny to shreds. We'll not let that happen."

"No, we can't."

"They're coming for us," Ruthie explains. "Taking control of the grandstand is no coincidence. They mean to drive our circus away."

"But why? You're a national hero!"

She takes my hand and leads me through the shadows. "Because I have a French name, and employ mostly immigrants, with the exception of Captain Merriman. These hooded creeps are looking for publicity."

"Let's give them some," I say, an idea blossoming. "But not the publicity they want."

Ruthie gives me a look. "What do you have in mind?"

I explain my idea, expecting her to scoff. Instead she grins a fierce, defiant grin, and says, "That just might work! I like the way you think, young man!"

———

Ten minutes later we're sneaking into the agricultural exhibits area. "Sneaking" because we don't know who to trust. Most of the farmers are good and kindly folks, but as we've seen, a significant number are either supporting the Klan from the sidelines, or have proudly donned the robes. So, our mission must remain secret.

We arrive at Big Boy's stall. The prizewinning bull is huge and intimidating. He lowers his head, eyes smoldering, and scuffs the turf with his hoof, as if to say, *Open the gate and I'll run you down.* Strangely enough, neither the owner nor the stable boy are present, leaving the mighty bull unguarded. Maybe they have been drawn to the grandstands by the hateful language.

Doesn't matter. We're not about to steal Big Boy. What we have in mind is something very different, but we do need the bull's help, so to speak.

Moving gingerly, we enter the stall. Big Boy stands his ground, massive head lowered, but does not attempt to butt us.

I remain terrified.

Ruthie takes a folded burlap bag from her jacket pocket and shakes it out. "Shovel?" she asks.

We are some distance from the grandstands, but not far enough to escape fragments of the Klansman's ranting speech.

"Filthy immigrants replacing our white nation!"

And the cheers and chants supporting him:

"K! K! K!"

"Turn back the tide! Take back our rightful heritage!"

"K! K! K!"

Ruthie grips me by the shoulder. "Ignore that poison," she implores me. "We are better than this, I promise! I have traveled all over this country, and I know in my heart we're better than this."

I nod. "It's my country, too."

"Remember that," she urges. "No matter what happens."

"Let's get this over with," I say, my voice thick with emotion.

For the first time since the white hoods flooded the grandstands, I am not afraid.

Ruthie holds the burlap bag open while I shovel it full, trying not to breathe through my nose.

26. *The Big Stink*

IT'S A LONG haul from Big Boy's stable to the airfield.
Me and Ruthie hold the bulging burlap bag between us
as we go, quick as we can manage. Trying not to breathe
through our noses because the stench is overpowering.
My eyes are watering so bad I can barely see. Not that I'd
know where I'm going, even if my eyes were clear.

Luckily, Ruthie has it all in her head, the shortest way.
She could find her path in the dark, if need be, but this is
broad daylight. Various people notice us on the midway,
dragging the smelly sack, but no one thinks to stop us, or
to ask what we have in mind. Probably they don't want to
know, and just want to steer clear of the mighty stench.

The King of the Klan is still shouting his poison into
the giant megaphone, a hate that carries to the midway
and out into the world.

Ruthie rolls her eyes. "Davy, pay this man no heed! His hate comes of fear and ignorance."

"Whatever you say."

She stops, looking at me curiously. "Davy?"

"He doesn't sound afraid," I respond hotly. "More like he enjoys making *us* afraid."

She tugs at the burlap bag and nods in agreement. "You have a point, young man. Let's get on with it!"

Finally, we limp onto the airfield. The flying circus crew is standing guard over the motor vehicles and the precious biplanes, without which there is no flying circus. Captain Merriman, Tony Martini, Lily Bash, Elsie Belinski, Maggie Mangano, Ronan O'Ryan, and Patrice Boudreau. Patrice with a rake slung over his shoulder like a rifle. O'Ryan holding a tire iron, smacking it softly into his open palm. Mrs. Mangano with a kitchen knife near as big as she is, and a gleam in her eye that says, *Be careful. Be very careful.* And my sister, Jo, of course, wearing her new leather pilot helmet, with the goggles loose about her neck. She gives me a nod of approval, as if she knows what Ruthie and I have in mind.

Maybe she does. She always was a good guesser.

"*La grande puzza!*" Tony Martini says, eyeing the reeking sack. "The big stink!"

Captain Merriman strides forward and embraces Ruthie. "My darling, I was worried they'd got you."

She looks partway embarrassed and partway pleased to be called his darling. News to me. Whatever grown-ups get up to, they're not likely to share with kids my age.

Jo says, "Davy, are you okay?"

"I'm aces."

"Good," she says. "Good."

That's when I know, from the quaver in her voice, that my big sister is as worried as me about what the Klan might do.

Ruthie says, "Ray? Did you find that map?"

The war hero nods curtly and unfurls a large map on the hood of Ruthie's Cadillac. He stabs a finger at a spot. "Our present location," he says bluntly. "As you know, I think we should leave immediately, before we are destroyed. I believe they mean to burn us out. I have seen hooded thugs with tins of kerosene. They claim it's to light their torches, but I haven't seen any torches."

"Understood," Ruthie says. She places a finger on a spot at the edge of the map. "Here," she says. "The New Hope Farm, owned by an old friend, the widow Madeline LaChance. Mrs. LaChance has offered us a place to lie low for a few days."

"God bless her," Ronan O'Ryan says reverently, making the sign of the cross.

"Fifty miles by road," Ruthie announces. "Less by air. Tony, Ryan, Patrice. Commit this map to memory. And drive like your lives depend on it. Our rendezvous shall be the New Hope Farm! Captain Merriman, Elsie, it will be a bumpy landing, in Madeline's cow pasture. But you have both made far more difficult landings. And this time Captain Merriman will have Jo in the passenger cockpit, watching and learning."

Captain Merriman salutes her.

Ruthie waves her hand dismissively. "None of that! We are a team, never forget it!"

"And you? Will you risk everything?" he wants to know, an expression of deep concern on his handsome face.

Ruthie stands ramrod straight. "If we let them get the best of us, they'll never stop. They'll ruin every show, every venue. That's not going to happen, not if me and Davy have anything to say about it!"

27. *Know That I Was There*

OUR LITTLE AIRFIELD instantly transforms into bus-
tling activity, now that we have our orders. The men will
see to it that the over-the-road vehicles escape the wrath
of the Klan. With Patrice behind the wheel of the big red
Cadillac, and Mrs. Mangano in the passenger seat, woe
to any hooded villain who attempts to stop them!

Tony and Ronan roar off in their racing vehicles, car
and motorcycle, kicking up rooster tails of dust. The Klan's
white charger may be impressive, dressed in its own silks,
but no horse is a match for a Bugatti Grand Prix, not with
a fearless daredevil at the wheel.

"Hurry!" Ruthie urges me. "They'll figure it out soon
enough. We don't have much time!"

There's no stopping Ruthie once she's on a mission,
and our mission is to drive the Ku Klux Klan from the

fairgrounds, or at least cut them down to size.

Ruthie grabs a fistful of rope and rigs the stinking sack of bull pucky to the side of the front cockpit.

"Perfect!" She hands me one of Maggie's kitchen knives. "Careful, this is as sharp as a surgical scalpel."

Then she picks me up and drops me into the front cockpit of the biplane. Boom, just like that, as if I weighed no more than a dog. Seeing my eyes widen, she laughs. "What did you think, silly? I can't do this on my own. It's your idea—you must help me make it happen."

I'm not sure if it's the eye-watering stink, or the shock of surprise. My original idea didn't involve me being along for the ride. Whatever, I can't find the words to complain as she buckles the shoulder harness around my skinny chest. "You'll be fine," she assures me. "Flying is in the family blood, whether you know it or not."

She confers briefly with Captain Merriman and Elsie. Soon all three biplanes are coughing to life, propellers whirring. Soon we're bumping across the grassy airfield, gathering speed.

Did you know airplanes shake with vibration just before taking off? Neither did I, and it scares me halfway to death. What if the struts come undone and the machine falls apart? What if the propeller spits me out like a cocktail onion?

What if, what if?

David Louis Michaud, stop asking scary questions if you don't want to hear the answers! I'm hanging on to Mrs. Mangano's kitchen knife with both hands so I don't cut myself, and with one last terrifying bump we're floating.

That's what it feels like, floating. Rising into the sunlight as Captain Merriman follows, tipping his wings like a gentleman waving goodbye. Jo gives a thumbs-up from the passenger cockpit. Once we're a few hundred feet in the air Captain Merriman peels away, climbing into the misty clouds. Elsie follows, vanishing into the mist. Heading, I assume, for the safe spot on the map.

Ruthie is climbing, too, at full throttle. The Jenny seems to rise without effort. Up, up we go, clear of the clouds, until all I can see is blue sky and below us a few patches of green. Just when my stomach's about to come out my mouth, Ruthie levels off and grins at me from the rear cockpit.

"Are you ready, Davy?" She shouts to be heard above the engine. "Hang on, my boy! You can tell this to your grandchildren!"

She jams the stick forward and suddenly we're diving. Diving straight down, or so it seems, with the earth spinning beneath us.

Below us the ground rushes up, much too fast. We can't possibly survive. The biplane will fall apart. The wings will fold up and we'll be crushed like bugs into a small, flaming hole in the ground.

"READY!" Ruthie roars. "USE BOTH HANDS!"

The speed of descent—surely we're falling from the sky!—pushes me back against the seat rest. The grandstand suddenly looms beneath us. We're dropping like a rock into a pond of upturned faces. Men in robes, peeling off their hoods to look up in astonishment. Farmers suddenly afraid, trying to get away. And still we dive, faster and faster.

Straight at the King of the Klan, the fat-headed man with the yellow hair and the pale blue eyes, aiming the giant megaphone at us, as if his hateful words can bring us down. Words drowned by the scream of the descending engine and the high-pitched whine of the propeller.

What was I thinking? We can't possibly survive. I'm praying that I'll never know what hit me—it'll be over in an instant—when Ruthie shouts, "NOW, DAVY, NOW!"

My hands have a mind of their own. They lift the knife, cutting through the rope like butter, releasing the noxious burlap bag of Big Boy's droppings, which falls like a bomb. Ruthie drags back on the stick, groaning with effort, and the Jenny responds, rising out of the dive just in time to clear the top of the grandstand.

Grandchildren, if you ever come to exist, know that I was there when the bag of prize bull poop exploded at the feet of the King Kleagle of the Ku Klux Klan, in the state of Maine, covering his magnificent white robe with a stinking brown mess!

28. *The Amazing Josephine*

FOR THE NEXT three days, we take refuge at New Hope Farm. Our airplanes and vehicles have been hidden behind the dairy barns, for the Klan is strong in these parts and might take notice.

The widow, Madeline LaChance, seems glad of the company. Although she has an accent from her birthplace in Quebec Province, some fifty miles to the north, her English is quite good. "A flying circus in our barns! *Quelle surprise!* My Armand would be so happy!"

Armand being her late husband, a lumberjack who carved pastures out of deep forest, one tree at a time, and against all odds made a dairy farm in the northern hills. They have three grown sons who work the farm and keep it pristine. One of them, Paul, brings the newspapers down from Jackman, the nearest village. The papers are filled with stories about what happened at the Skowhegan Fairgrounds.

FAMED AVIATRIX SAYS BULL! TO THE KKK
GRAND KLEAGLE SHOWERED WITH STINK BOMB
KLAN VOWS VENGENCE

Our airborne response to the Klan is the biggest story in the state and, according to the wireless, has gone nationwide.

SOUTHERN KLAN CALLS UPON
NORTHERN BROTHERS TO RETALIATE

As Jo explains, the reaction is both bad and good. Good because we humiliated the local Klan leader. Bad for the same reason.

"They'll be out for revenge," Jo confides. "Captain Merriman says we must post guards. He wants to end the season early, to be safe."

"What does Ruthie say?"

Jo smiles. "Let's just say she's not in a quitting state of mind."

Not surprisingly, the crew treats our time at the farm as a holiday to be celebrated. Captain Merriman may have posted an armed guard (Patrice, equipped with a war surplus Enfield rifle), but the daredevils can't be stopped from risking their lives for the thrill of it. Forbidden from the circus vehicles and from flying and racing, they invent a game they call Walking the Beam.

The game is played in the hay barn, which smells wonderfully of mowed grass and rich earth. A sturdy beam of white oak spans thirty feet, from the hayloft to the opposite wall, at a height of twelve feet above the hard oak floor. The beam is about eight inches wide, and the goal is to walk from the hayloft to the wall and back without falling. I say walk, but none of them walks. They strut blindfolded like Tony Martini, or they walk on their hands like Lily Bash, or skip gaily like Elsie Belinski, or backward like Ronan O'Ryan, tipping his hat. He's a mechanic, not a daredevil, but that doesn't stop him from trying to impress Lily, who applauds his every step.

Jo can't resist joining in the fun. She dances across the beam and back, kicking her heels and slapping her ankles, as they all clap and sing "The Charleston." She makes it look so easy, as if the narrow beam were as wide as a ball-room floor.

My big sister. I've known her all my life, but I never knew she had it in her to sing and dance and entertain. Must be that she kept it hidden away. Or maybe it was our life in the tenements, just scraping by, with no place for skylarking. It was something she kept to herself because Mama needed her to be a certain way. Serious, studious, dutiful. Now here she is, showing off her talent and nerve. She's so happy and carefree I can't be afraid for her. That confident grin tells me she knows what she's doing.

She's becoming the Amazing Josephine, and it's a beautiful thing to see.

29. *Never Surrender*

ON THE THIRD day, the fun and games come to a sudden end. At dusk, three Klansmen arrive on horseback. Their robes have the look of bedsheets rather than fine satin, and the hoods might be pillowcases. Their horses are farm horses, plodding and sturdy.

"Locals," says Mrs. LaChance, glancing through the kitchen window. Her nose wrinkles in disgust. "Neighbors. Dairy farmers like us. They should be ashamed."

Patrice steps into view, leveling his Enfield at the masked horsemen. If they are impressed or fearful they do not show it, nor do they back away. Next thing, our hostess bolts out of the house and confronts them herself. We can't hear the conversation, but when the horsemen finally depart and she returns to the kitchen, Mrs. LaChance appears stricken. As if wounded by some invisible, terrible weapon.

"I can't believe it. I know those men and they know me. Makes no difference, they will destroy us out of spite."

Ruthie looks grim. "Madeline, you must tell me exactly what they have threatened to do."

Mrs. LaChance shakes her head. Tears stream from her eyes. "It is too shameful."

Eventually Ruthie persuades her to tell the whole story. Turns out her fellow farmers, recent Klan converts, threatened to ban the farm from the dairy co-op that buys their milk, so long as they harbor what the Klansmen call "our enemy." Meaning Ruthie Reynard and her flying circus.

With no place to sell milk, New Hope Farm is bound to fail, and sooner rather than later.

I have never seen Ruthie so truly angry. Her eyes grow still and cold. "This is my fault," she says through clenched teeth. "I know what these hate-filled people are capable of doing, and yet I taunted them. I humiliated them. And this is the price we pay. That my dearest friends be ruined!"

Captain Merriman looks as solemn as if attending a funeral. What he feared has come to pass, although he is too much of a gentleman to say "I told you so." Instead he clears his throat and gently announces, "Mrs. LaChance, we thank you for your kindness and your hospitality, but we can't let ourselves be the source of your distress. If Ruthie is agreed, we'll pack up and be gone at first light."

Ruthie agrees, and then orders us all to our improvised bunk room in the hay barn. Once we are assembled, she asks for silence.

"I will be brief. We're all in this together and what happens next must be put to a vote. As I see it, we have two options. One: Shut down the show and slink away with our tails between our legs. Two: We carry on for the last few weeks of the season, provided Captain Merriman can find sufficient security to keep us safe. So, what is your choice, quit or carry on?"

We erupt as one. "Carry on!"

"Good!" Ruthie's grin is pure sunshine, lifting our spirits. "We fly tomorrow. The ground may belong to those who hate, but we own the sky!"

We cheer, "Ruthie! Ruthie! Ruthie!"

"NEVER SURRENDER!" she roars, raising a clenched fist.

30. *It Comes Out of Left Field*

I'VE HEARD OF Pinkerton agents—everybody has—but had never seen one in the flesh. From the pulp magazine stories, you'd think they were ten feet tall. A private army of investigators armed to the teeth, able to outsmart even the craftiest criminal. In reality, as we soon discovered, agents of the Pinkerton National Detective Agency don't look like anything special. They are average men in suits and hats who seem a little bored to be protecting a troupe of daredevils. They are polite with Ruthie, of course, but don't seem much impressed by her death-defying exploits.

Maybe we're not up to their famous standards, like tracking Jesse James, and Butch Cassidy and the Sundance Kid, or being featured in Sherlock Holmes stories. Never mind, Captain Merriman, who hired them, made sure the

Klan knows there are armed agents guarding every air show.

"Ruthie says they'll make the hood-wearing hoodlums think twice," Jo says. "Everybody knows Pinkertons will not hesitate to shoot, and that they can call in reinforcements if necessary."

The Klan is raging across the state, holding marches and signing up new members by the thousands. There are reports of Catholic church and Jewish temple fires, and crosses burning in immigrant neighborhoods, but none have showed themselves to us since that threatening visit to the New Hope Farm.

For the next few weeks, the Ruthie Reynard Flying Circus will be "skipping fields," as Ruthie puts it. Bringing the show to small towns and villages, most of which do not have grandstands, let alone proper fairgrounds. Folks gather in a grassy field, sometimes at a dirt track, watch our daredevils risk their lives, and then it is on to the next place. That means more work for all of us because we'll be packing up every day or two.

Maybe it's the constant moving from place to place that makes me worry about when the season is over. When the biplanes are grounded and the members of the circus go their separate ways.

"Jo, what will happen to us? Do we go back to Biddeford?"

My sister shrugs. She doesn't seem particularly worried. "Ruthie pledged to make sure we're okay."

"Yes, but what if that splits us up, Jo? What if she sends me off to the home for boys?"

Jo senses my alarm and her attitude softens. "Oh, Davy, you worry too much. We'll stay together no matter what. You and I are family and that will never change."

"You promise?"

Her answer is to give me a fierce hug.

After talking with Jo, I'm less worried and anxious, more wondering what happens next. When it does happen, it comes out of left field and will change my sister's life.

31. *My Dearest Darling Wonderful Friends*

THE PINKERTON AGENTS might not be terribly impressed by our derrings-do and death-defying stunts, but they are dazzled by Mrs. Mangano's cooking and never miss a meal. Why, only the other day I witnessed one of the beefier men demolish an entire spiced ham, followed by a large tray of cannoli and a half gallon of milk. Sweet Maggie does not mind. She would feed the entire world if it were in her power.

Jo and I are watching the same man devour a chafing dish of slow-grilled sausages. So far, fifteen jumbo sausages—and yes, I've been counting.

"Honestly," Jo says, keeping her voice low, "if Pinkertoning ever gets too dull, he could join a sideshow. People would pay to watch him eat, on the chance he might explode."

I laugh so hard I'm sneezing milk when Tony Martini strides into the tent, looking worried. He wants to know if we've seen Ronan the mechanic or Lily Bash.

We shake our heads. "Not since last night at supper," Jo says.

"I check by his cot. His trunk is gone!"

On the road as we are, our belongings—clothing and such—are kept in leather trunks so there's no need to pack up for each move.

"What about Lily's trunk?" I ask.

Tony shakes his head. "No, no. Never do I enter the lady tent. Is forbidden." He grabs a mug of coffee from the urn and joins us at our table. "I have my suspicion," he says, rolling his eyes. "Is *amore*, maybe. Love."

The daredevil's guess is confirmed a few minutes later when Ruthie enters, holding up a letter. "For those who don't already know, Lily and Ronan have eloped." She reads: "'My dearest darling wonderful friends, by the time you read this, my love and I will be on the first train to Boston. Ronan has family in that city, and that is where we will make a new life. Ruthie, I am finally and happily grounded! Please wish us luck, and accept our apologies for our sudden departure.'"

Ruthie looks a bit grim. "I'm afraid this particular love story has deprived us, not only of a wing walker, but of a skilled mechanic. I have consulted with Captain Merriman, who will attempt to replace Mr. O'Ryan. As for Lily Bash, she's irreplaceable."

With that, she marches out of the tent.

"What did Lily mean, she's 'happily grounded'?" I ask.

Jo shrugs. "I'm not sure, but it sounds like she has given up her life in the air for a life on the ground. I wish her luck. And good luck to Ronan if he tries to boss her around!"

"But why run away in the middle of the night?"

"Because eloping is much more dramatic, and Lily loves a good show. And maybe they were afraid Ruthie would talk them out of it. It doesn't matter. What's done is done."

Oddly enough, my sister seems happy that we've lost our famous wing walker.

32. The Test

AS I FEARED, Jo wants Lily's job.

At first, Ruthie won't hear of it. "There's no doubt you have the skill and the nerve," she says. "But you are my ward. I am responsible for your health and safety."

Jo never raises her voice, but she won't back down. "You were responsible for Lily's health and safety, too," she reminds Ruthie. "I know there is risk and I accept it. I am eighteen and entitled to make my own decisions. My decision is to become a wing walker."

"Josephine." Ruthie sounds exasperated.

"Hear me out. Please? I've studied Lily's moves for weeks and weeks. I know every step she takes and in what order. Where the handholds are located. How best to keep my balance. How to compensate for wind flow. I can do it, you know I can."

Ruthie sighs. "My dear girl, you are like a dog with a bone. You won't give up."

"I learned that from you," Jo says with a grin. "Ruthie, let me help. Please! I shall not fail you!"

Arms crossed, Ruthie thinks it over and finally nods her okay. "No inverted runs. Lily trained ten months before attempting the upside-down stunt."

Jo agrees. "Just the wings, right-side up. I'll be safe."

———

In the afternoon, Jo climbs aboard the Jenny. Ruthie takes off from a bumpy field and heads for a nearby lake. She told me what she had in mind, in case I want to observe. The very idea makes me nervous, but how can I not watch my sister walk on wings?

The Jenny slowly circles over the lake at a low altitude, no more than fifty feet above the water. This is how Ruthie teaches all her wing walkers, she explained. If they fall while learning, there's every chance of surviving, assuming they can swim. Which Jo can. She waves to me from the front cockpit, and the next moment she steps out onto the lower wing. Moving confidently among the struts and wires that keep the contraption from collapsing under the stress of flight.

She seems so sure of herself that I forget to be afraid. One hand clinging to a wing strut, she waves again. I assume she's waving at me, but then I get it. She's pretending to wave to the crowds, to her adoring fans! She turns toward Ruthie and makes a little bow, and then a salute to her pilot. Even from my ground-level view, it's obvious that Ruthie is laughing out loud.

Using hand signals, Ruthie directs her to the middle of the lower wing, halfway between the cockpit and the wingtip. Jo braces herself between two of the struts. What had been a smooth, slow flight suddenly changes. Ruthie waggles the wings, as if she's trying to throw Jo off balance.

Jo tips and sways between the struts, as if maintaining her balance on the deck of a ship in heavy seas. Ruthie responds by dipping the wings until she's flying almost sideways. Still Jo keeps her balance, no matter what Ruthie does with the Jenny. If she loses her grip she'll end up in the pond, and that might very well mean the end of her wing-walking adventure: Ruthie would never risk losing her over solid ground.

My big sister can't be shaken loose from her perch on the lower wing. She has passed the test! Ruthie signals for her return to the cockpit, and when she's belted in, the Jenny circles the bumpy field and lands precisely where it took off. Rubber tires bouncing, tail dragging in the grass.

I make a beeline to the biplane and arrive in time to give Jo a hand down from the cockpit.

"I did it, Davy! I did it, I did it!"

She gives me a hug that squeezes the breath right out of me. "This is the best day ever, little brother. The very best!"

Ruthie takes off her flying helmet and goggles, shakes out her hair, and give me a long, serious look. A look that says the fun and games are over.

"So, what do you think?" she asks me. "Are you okay with this?"

After a moment, I respond. "Whatever Jo wants to do, I'm all for it."

What I don't know is that in a few days the Amazing Josephine will be almost as famous as Lily Bash.

33. A Big Surprise

WHEN AUGUST WANES, and school beckons, Ruthie arranges what she calls a deferment. Farm kids often delay school until the last harvest is in, and Ruthie wants me to stay on for the next few weeks, even if it means she must tutor me herself.

What I love about this arrangement is that Ruthie's idea of teaching is to hand me a book. "Read this and we'll discuss" is how she puts it. Which is way, way better than school. I get to read *The Jungle Book* and *20,000 Leagues Under the Sea* and the Oz books, and there's no homework involved!

And best of all, no so-called boarding school for boys, at least for now.

The first week of September, our flying circus sets up camp at the fairgrounds in Cumberland. The harness-racing track is perfect for Tony Martini and his Bugatti, which spews up an impressive cloud of dust as he skids through the turns. Ruthie chases him in her Jenny, keeping the wingtips just high enough to clear the ground.

Every turn is dangerous, but also exciting.

"THEY'RE COMING AROUND THE LAST TURN! IT'S NECK AND NECK IN THE HOMESTRETCH!"

The crowd stands, cheering them on.

"GO, RUTHIE, GO! GO, RUTHIE, GO!"

The race car and the Jenny zoom past the grandstands.

"IT'S RUTHIE REYNARD BY A WHISKER!"

Moments later, *Liberty Belle* flashes by, at an altitude of three hundred feet and an airspeed in excess of two hundred miles an hour.

"LADIES AND GENTLEMEN, IF YOU BLINKED YOU MISSED IT! THAT WAS ELSIE BELL, THE FASTEST FEMALE ALIVE!"

Pinkerton agents range along the bottom of the stands, watching the audience, not the air show. So far, so good: no hooded men, no threats. Just a rowdy crowd enjoying itself, cheering on the brave performers.

In a new development, Captain Merriman has hired a local band. Trumpet, clarinet, drums, and ragtime piano! They've been playing popular tunes in between events. "King Porter Stomp," "It Had to Be You," "Limehouse Blues." All lively, and easy for the crowd to sing along with the band. Not me. I've got a voice like a pond frog and don't care to share it.

I ask the captain when Jo will make her appearance.

He gives me a sly smile and says, "We're saving the best for last."

"No upside-down stunts, right?"

"Right-side up, but with a big surprise."

"What? Wait! What kind of surprise?"

He sees how worried I am and gives me a reassuring smile. "A safe kind, Davy. It's something that's never been done before. Your sister came up with it herself, and I was called in to rig the aircraft for her safety."

I pester him a bit, but he won't say more.

"Hey, popcorn!"

The crowd is hungrier than usual, or maybe Maggie's popcorn is especially well buttered. Passing the little paper sacks along and collecting the returning nickels keeps me busy. I miss Patrice and Tony doing their all-in-the-timing hat stunt because I'm handing out popcorn at exactly that instant. The astonished cheers from the crowd tell me the moment the hat is snatched and Patrice is safe from the whirling propeller.

Next, Ruthie and Captain Merriman have their exciting mock dogfight, which today ends with black smoke streaming from the captain's Jenny. A harmless smoke bomb, of course. All part of putting on a good show, or as Ruthie says, "giving value for money."

After the dogfight, I hurry back to Maggie's tent for the next batch. As I'm climbing into the stands with a full carrier of popcorn, the announcer shouts into his giant megaphone.

"LADIES AND GENTLEMEN! CHILDREN OF ALL AGES! CAST YOUR EYES TO THE EAST! YOU ARE ABOUT TO WITNESS THE FIRST STUNT PER-FORMED BY OUR NEW WING WALKER! PLEASE WELCOME . . . THE AMAZING JOSEPHINE!"

Ruthie's biplane comes up over the horizon, heading straight for the center of the grandstands. She turns smoothly, and suddenly Jo is out on the wing, between the struts.

The newly hired band erupts into the hottest song-and-dance craze in the country, maybe the world: "The Charleston."

And Jo dances on the wings of the biplane.

She dances exactly as she danced upon the beam in the barn at New Hope Farm. Kicking up her heels and slap-ping them with her hands, rocking back and forth to the lively music. Grinning with the fun of it, two hundred feet in the air. As casual and confident as if she were safe on a dance floor.

The crowd roars in approval. Not cheers, not shouts, it ROARS as one, astonished by my amazing sister. A poor girl from a mill town, the orphaned daughter of immigrants, but in this mighty moment, a new star in the sky.

We all sing along, even the popcorn boy:

Charleston! Charleston! Made in Carolina
Some dance, some prance,
I'll say, there's nothing finer
Than the Charleston, Charleston.

Then, somehow, we're all chanting to the famous tune, with our own words:

JO-SE-PHINE A-MAZ-ING JO-SE-PHINE!

If only they knew. My big sister was amazing long before she stepped out on that wing.

34. *The New Sensation*

THE NEXT DAY the crowds double in size. At first the news of the dancing wing walker spreads by word of mouth. By the third performance, newspaper photographers are setting their cameras on tripods, competing for pictures of the newest sensation in the world of daredevil aviation.

Over the last few years, all kinds of stunts have been performed on the wings of airplanes. Parachute jumps. Mock sword fights between costumed pirates. Handstands, tennis matches, boxing matches. But my big sister is the first to wing dance that happy, jubilant dance they call the Charleston.

Jo gives credit to Captain Merriman for hiring the band. "The live music makes it work," she says. "The band sets hearts to racing. Everybody knows the tune and has tried to learn the dance. It's the biggest craze ever. All I'm doing is taking it into the sky, and making it look dangerous."

"That's because it is," I insist.

"Not really. It's all part of the illusion," she says. "I'll prove it. Follow me!"

We head to the flying machines, parked in the grass.

"This is the secret that keeps me safe. Tell no one!"

Jo shows me the safety harness rigged by Captain Merriman. The harness part is little more than a leather belt. Belt buckle in front, with a steel ring protruding through the leather in the back. Attached to the ring is a six-foot length of thin, high-strength wire that is firmly attached to the frame of the biplane. Jo is already wearing the safety belt when she leaps out of the cockpit onto the wing.

"If I lose my balance, the worst that can happen is a bad bruise from the narrow belt. I won't be plummeting to the ground, no matter what."

"Unless the wire breaks."

She shakes her head. "This is special braided wire, rated to five hundred pounds. I weigh a hundred and five."

"Okay," I say doubtfully.

Smiling, she says, "Oh, Davy. I'm so lucky to have a brother who worries about my well-being! There are some daredevils who take terrible risks and pay with their lives. I'm not one of them, and neither is Ruthie. We take all reasonable precautions. We're putting on a thrilling show, but it's a show, okay? We make it look more dangerous than it actually is."

"So, you can't fall, no matter what?"

"Exactly right. Please stop worrying about me. I know what I'm doing. Promise?"

"I promise." I put my hand to my heart as a pledge. "I'm really proud to be your brother, Jo. I point up and tell them the dancing girl is my sister and their eyes get big."

"Really?"

"The girls want to be you, and the boys want to be with you."

"David Michaud!" She's blushing, but not really mad.

"It's what the announcer said to the crowd, and they all cheered," I explain. Then, more seriously, "Is it fun being the new sensation? Do you like it?"

Jo folds her arms across her chest and shakes her head. "No, little brother, I don't like it. I love it!"

35. *Terrible Silence*

DISASTER STRIKES ON a sunny afternoon in early autumn. A few of the red maples have begun to turn. There's a forest of them clustered along the north end of the fairgrounds. The red maples make a pretty background for Ruthie's mock dogfight with Captain Merriman.

Autumn leaves like specks of blood, glinting in the sunlight.

"Popcorn! Hey, popcorn!"

My back is turned, but I can hear the RAT-A-TAT-TAT of the "machine guns" installed on the biplanes. Simple but realistic. Hand crank a spring, flip the lever, RAT-A-TAT-TAT, complete with puffs of gun smoke. The crowd cheers wildly.

The announcer screams: *"NO! NO! CAN IT BE?*

CAPTAIN MERRIMAN HAS BEEN HIT! HE'S GOING DOWN!"

It's the same at every show, but still I sneak a look, just to be sure. Merriman's Jenny is in a steep dive, trailing smoke. All part of the stunt. At the last possible moment, he pulls out of the dive, skimming above the trees. We all cheer.

The biggest thrill you can deliver, Ruthie says, is to make them think you can't possibly survive, and then survive with style. They love you for it. They don't want to see anyone die, not really. Not most of them.

I wonder. Those Klansmen who showed their faces had the look of men who might enjoy watching someone die. Especially if that someone happened to be other than so-called Anglo-Saxons. Black, French, Italian, Russian, Polish, Jew, Native American, take your pick. If any one of them go down in flames, or find themselves at the end of a rope, the Klan would cheer, of this I am sure.

Ruthie executes a wide turn. She's heading back for a triumphant pass, having won the "dogfight." Just as she comes out of the turn, beyond the trees, her engine sputters and dies.

Silence. Terrible silence. Then a gasp from the crowd when they realize this isn't a stunt, but an actual disaster in the making. I put my hand to my mouth, shocked beyond reason. How can this be? Surely, she will crash. Without power to make it fly, her Jenny plummets out of sight, behind the trees.

Trembling, I wait for the explosion as she smashes into the forest. The waiting hurts, like a punch to the stomach. I want to shout or scream, but nothing comes out.

Then the Jenny reappears, gliding just above the treetops. With no engine noise, we hear the air whistling through the rigging.

Wild cheering erupts.

"GO, RUTHIE! GO, RUTHIE! GO! GO! GO!"

I can't join in. Fear has closed my throat, stopped my breath. She's never going to make it. The blood-tinged maples look like claws trying to snatch her from the sky and turn her biplane into flaming kindling. By some miracle of expertise and skill, Ruthie keeps a few feet above the trees. But she can't defy the pull of gravity, and at the very edge of the maple forest, the tail skeg bounces through the questing branches. The plane tips forward, heading straight down into the ground just beyond the forest.

Doom. Impossible to avoid. But no! The only impossible thing is the astonishing maneuver from the ace pilot, who somehow twists the biplane back to horizontal and lands safely, bouncing hard but staying in one piece.

The crowd roars with relief. We all rush forward, cheering as we run across the track, through the meadow, eager to greet our hero. She climbs down from the rear cockpit and stands there with one hand on the plane that very nearly killed her.

Captain Merriman reaches her first. He picks her up and swings her around, a big grin of relief on his face.

"There's only one pilot in the world who could pull that off!" he cries out. "Ruthie Reynard, you are amazing!"

36. Sydney Barnes to the Rescue

WHEN AT LAST the adoring crowd has dispersed, Ruthie gathers us together. We're all somber, especially Elsie, who very nearly saw her hero perish.

Ruthie does not disagree. "Make no mistake, I came within an inch of destroying the aircraft, and possibly myself. There's half a tank of fuel, enough to burn that forest to the ground. This engine has never before failed me. We'll need to find out exactly what happened before we can continue."

Captain Merriman clears his throat. "The new mechanic is due to arrive today."

Ruthie nods. "Good. He's needed now more than ever."

Sydney Barnes, the new mechanic, strides onto the field within the hour. To be honest, he looks more like a daredevil than a mechanic. Compact, broad shouldered, he has a remarkable mustache and a twinkle in his brown eyes. The mustache curls out wider than his head, held in place by deftly applied wax.

Sydney hails from Chicago and has that broad way of talking. He's friendly and likes joking around, even with kids.

"Take a good look, kiddos. What you see before you is the bee's knees of aviation mechanics," he says, thumping his chest. "I ain't no dewdropper."

"What's a dewdropper?" I ask.

"Same as a lollygagger. A lazy good for nothing. Speaking of which, I best get to work. Time's a wasting!"

Jokes are fun, but when it comes to finding out how the Jenny almost killed Ruthie, he's deadly serious. He lets me hang around while he removes the cowling and crawls up on the V-8 engine to inspect it.

Sydney strokes his impressive mustache and winks at me. "Mechanic has to know an engine like he knows his own face in the mirror," he says.

I'm not sure what that means, exactly. But maybe it helped him find the problem, which he does in less than five minutes. Sniffing at the carburetor as he fiddles with the throttle, he announces, "Got it! Would you be kind enough to let Miss Reynard know?"

I race off to find Ruthie. She marches up to the Jenny and says, "Well?"

"Shellac. Very distinctive smell." He grins and smooths his mustache. "Have a sniff yourself."

She does so and reacts sharply. "Somebody spiked the fuel!"

"Must have. Shellac will do it. Gums up the carburetor."

"Sabotage," Ruthie says, looking fierce. "Somebody wants me dead."

Sydney nods thoughtfully. "It would appear so. I understand you have enemies in a certain organization."

Ruthie folds her arms across her chest. I've never seen her looking so worried and unhappy. "Unfortunately, I do. What I need to find out is how whoever did this got past the guards." She gestures at the exposed engine. "Can you fix it?"

Sydney wipes his hands on a rag and smiles encouragingly. "No problem, Miss Reynard, I'll drain the fuel and scour the tank. Carb needs rebuilding. I'll get right on it, remove the shellac residue with solvents. She'll be good as new."

"Thank you, Mr. Barnes. With your help, we'll get the circus back in the air."

"Happy to oblige."

Ruthie goes off to consult with Captain Merriman and the Pinkertons.

Sydney is as good as his word, completing the repairs that afternoon, in time for the next show. Ruthie pronounces herself satisfied that the engine runs as smoothly and reliably as it did before the sabotage.

"Cleared for takeoff!" she announces jubilantly.

The spectators at the Cumberland fairgrounds are eager for the show to start, delayed as it has been. They're also hungry for popcorn and hot dogs and peanuts in the shell. I'm not the only vendor in the stands, although sometimes it feels that way.

"Popcorn! Hey, popcorn!"

For a few hours every show day, popcorn is my whole world. The making of it, the bagging of it, the selling of it. It's not until the band launches into "The Charleston" that I look up to the sky, searching for my sister.

There she is, with the crowd roaring its amazement at the girl who dances so eagerly upon the delicate wings of Ruthie's biplane. As usual I'm thrilled, but always concerned for Jo's safety. Newly included in my list of things to worry about, that the engine might sputter and fail. What might happen after that I can't allow myself to imagine.

Too scary, too awful.

As for today, the wing-dancer stunt goes off without a

hitch, as do all the other acts. My costumed antics as Donkey Boy, the biplane race with the Bugatti, the rope trick, the hat trick, the dogfight, Elsie's amazing speed runs, and lastly, the flights through fireworks, with Ruthie and Captain Merriman firing Roman candles at each other. And making sure they miss. It all happens safely, without a problem. As if yesterday's near disaster was simply a bad dream, best forgotten.

I can't forget. I don't dare.

37. Men in the Shadows

THAT EVENING, AFTER a massive Maggie dinner, I duck outside for a chance to admire the autumn sunset, which coincides with the rising of a harvest moon. The scene looks like a painted postcard, only prettier.

I wander over to where the vehicles, land and air, have been parked in the meadow. Three Pinkerton agents stand vigil. Word is, Captain Merriman gave them a proper tongue-lashing about lack of security, for how else could the fuel be spiked? Klansmen may be many things, but they are not invisible.

It gives me comfort to think the bright light of the full moon will surely discourage any saboteurs. As I'm about to head back to the tent, Sydney Barnes slips into the meadow and strikes up a conversation with one of the Pinkertons. They seem to be on friendly terms.

Mr. Barnes is a very friendly fellow.

Nothing wrong with that, is there?

———

Tony has a new variation of the driverless car stunt. We try it out the next afternoon. Instead of going around the track once at high speed, Tony puts the Alfa Romeo into a power skid, making the car spin around on the far corner of the track. To the audience, it looks like the "donkey" lost control of the race car.

My job is to act like I'm mad. I leap out of the car and butt my donkey head on the rear bumper, trying to get it moving. When the car won't respond, I kick a tire and hobble away, doing my best donkey gallop.

Suddenly the grandstand erupts in laughter. I look back and discover that the car is following me. It goes when I go, stops when I stop. Donkey Boy becomes increasingly agitated, wagging his head in frustration. The more upset he gets, the more the crowd roars.

The act concludes when I remove the headpiece and take a bow.

"ALL HANDS TOGETHER FOR DAVID MICHAUD!"

By now I've been applauded scores of times, but it never gets old.

Minutes later I'm hidden away under one of the grandstands, folding up the costume and stowing it in the leather valise. That's when I happen to glimpse a couple of men in the shadows, similarly hidden under the grandstand. Their faces are in darkness, and the crowd noise makes it difficult to hear, but they seem to be speaking.

What are they saying that makes them want to hide in the shadows?

I crouch behind the Alfa Romeo, keeping out of sight. Could they be the men who sabotaged Ruthie's biplane? The men shift, conversation concluded, and pass briefly into a shaft of daylight coming through the seats above.

Sydney Barnes and a man who could be one of the bruisers who nearly assaulted Mrs. Mangano at the Union Fair.

———

"What do you mean 'could be'?" Jo demands.

"It was Sydney for sure. The other man was the right size, but I barely glimpsed his face. I can't be sure."

Jo nods thoughtfully. "Might be Sydney's bookie. There are horse races to wager on."

"They do that in broad daylight," I point out.

"Still, having a private conversation isn't a crime. Tell you what, little brother: We keep an eye on Mr. Barnes."

38. *Man on a Mission*

THAT'S HOW JO and I happen to be wide-awake at two in the morning, when everybody else is sound asleep. We're keeping an eye out for the man with the mustache, Sydney Barnes.

So far, not a creature is stirring.

We have reason to be suspicious, and not just because of his conversation in the shadows. Earlier in the day Jo learned that Mr. Barnes was in town the night the fuel tank was spiked. Tony Martini had seen him in the lobby of a hotel and remembered that remarkable mustache. Why would he bother with a hotel? Why not come directly to the circus, knowing we needed a mechanic and his expertise was wanted? Why wait until the following afternoon, after the engine failed and Ruthie narrowly avoided disaster?

"Maybe he has a girlfriend," Jo speculated. "Some sort of personal business that delayed his arrival."

"Maybe," I say. "Or maybe he's—"

Jo shushes me and points. Sydney Barnes has slipped out of his tent and is moving like a man on a mission.

We follow a good distance behind Mr. Barnes as he heads for the airfield. He's not trying to avoid being seen, with his head held high in the light of the full moon. Almost—and this sends chills up my spine—almost as if he wants to be seen.

Is he onto us? Does he know we've been watching him? For a second I consider turning back, but Jo silently urges that we continue. The biplanes look like sleeping birds in the hush of night. The air is summer warm, with a hint of autumn coming on. The only sounds are a few peepers from a nearby pond. That and the pounding of my heart.

Jo crouches behind the parked Bugatti, signaling that I do the same. We lift our heads slowly, sighting through the windshield to the biplanes beyond. The silent, sleeping Jennys and Elsie's sleek racer, supposedly under close guard by Pinkertons.

We watch as Sydney Barnes and one of the agents exchange salutes. One hand over the heart, fingers splayed, the other raised shoulder high and straight out.

"Oh my Lord," Jo whispers, astonished. "They're Klansmen."

39. *The Last Thing I See*

MY FIRST IMPULSE is to run, but Jo holds me back. Without speaking she makes me understand that we must stay hidden. Her eyes are huge in the moonlight. In them, I see fear, anger, and bafflement. How can it be that the mechanic hired to maintain our vehicles is himself a Klansmen? And what of the Pinkerton agent, pledged to protect us?

We are betrayed! Our crew has been infiltrated by men who despise us. I know in that moment, with a certainty right down to my bones, that Sydney Barnes intends to murder Ruthie Reynard by arranging an accident. An accident that might well involve my sister the wing walker, dancing to her death.

How dare they! Scared as I am, I want to grab a weapon, any weapon, and turn it upon the men who seek to harm us. At the same time, I am mindful that Pinkertons are armed with pistols and famously know how to use them. Only a few minutes ago the idea that their weapons might be turned upon us was unthinkable. Witnessing the Klan salute changes everything.

Our guards and protectors cannot be trusted. Ruthie must be warned!

Sydney Barnes and the Pinkerton laugh loudly, having shared some joke, no doubt at the expense of those they hold in contempt. Jo nudges me and points in the direction of the camp. We must make our way back and sound the alarm. Jo takes a deep breath and leads the way, crawling through the meadow grass on hands and knees. If we stand and run they will surely see us.

It's all I can do to keep from screaming at the two men. I feel their hatred like a hot poker in my belly. It makes me angry and afraid. The fear grows stronger as we crawl though the grass, desperately trying to be invisible.

I pray for clouds to block the full moon and keep us undiscovered. But the night sky remains clear and bright enough to cast dim shadows. We're making progress—the tents are in sight!—when black-booted feet stomp out of the grass and stop a yard from where we've halted.

I look up, and my heart nearly stops beating.

Sydney Barnes, grinning like he's found a wonderful

gift. "Looky looky, the little French fries are crawling like babies. Ain't this a sight?"

Another shadow looms. The Pinkerton agent, carrying rope.

"RUN!" I cry, leaping to my feet.

Striking faster than a rattlesnake, Barnes snatches me and Jo, clutching hold of us by our necks. Shaking us as he chuckles, delighted with himself. "You think you had me fooled? Me? I am a thousand times smarter than any Frenchie. Whatever you may be thinking with your feeble, lower-race brains, I did not come here to sabotage the aircraft. Not tonight, once I saw that you were both awake at so late an hour. My intention was to draw you away from the tents. I saw you'd been spying on me, and could easily be fooled into following."

I try to cry out, but his grip tightens, throttling my scream. Breathing becomes a problem.

"I figured it would be easy to do this if we got you alone."

Do this? My brain is fizzing. What's he talking about? I black out for a moment. By the time I wake up, the Pinkerton has roped us like cattle. Ankles and hands tied up, gags shoved in our mouths. I'm immensely grateful to be able to breathe through my nose, filling my fiery lungs.

"But this is your lucky day, my little French fries,"

Barnes sneers. "You're about to be useful for the first time in your sad, pathetic lives."

He picks Jo and me up by the ropes, carrying us like trussed-up luggage. It's hard to see what's going on, with our faces pointing to the ground. I catch a glimpse of the Pinkerton's shiny boots and then hear an automobile door being yanked open.

The rear door of a brand-new Packard Six.

"Upsy-daisy," Barnes says jauntily. He swings us through the car door and drops us to the floor. Wham! "I hear a peep out of you, I'll stomp you like a bug."

The last thing I see is a heavy blanket spreading out to hide us.

40. *Welcome to the Klavern*

IT FEELS LIKE I've been dropped into the Packard from a great height. Every part of me hurts, especially where the ropes are binding my wrists and ankles. Jo must hurt the same. We're lying in the back seat, half smothered by the blanket. My heart beats like hummingbird wings. But for the gag I would be screaming. We might as well be locked in a coffin, that's how close it is. Panic has me by the throat—I hate small spaces! Hate them! Can't breathe, can't think.

Stop it, Davy. You can't afford to panic; your lives may depend on being able to think clearly. Slow your breathing. Concentrate. Think, boy, think.

Why have we been abducted? Barnes sneered that we would be "useful." What does that mean? Can't be anything good. The Southern Klan murders innocent Blacks by lynching. Very often public lynching, attended by followers who urge them on.

Are we to be lynched, my sister and me? Has the Maine Klan decided to take up that practice and extend it to the hated immigrants? Will they torment us with their torches before stringing us up?

Between the thumping of my heart, I finally conclude that if they'd wanted to hang us from a tree, there were plenty available at the fairgrounds. Barnes and his fellow Klansmen must have something else in mind. Might be they are using us to avenge their King Kleagle, or whatever he calls himself. Maybe abducting us is a way of punishing Ruthie. Unless, of course, they intend to hold us for ransom.

I chew at the gag, trying to shred it with my front teeth. More than anything I want to speak to Jo. To see if she's okay, or if she has a plan to help us escape. How that would be accomplished, with the two of us trussed up like chickens for a roast, is beyond my imagining.

One thing I do know: My amazing sister will not give up. A woman so fearless she dances on airplane wings is not going to be intimidated by a snake like Sydney Barnes.

A corner of the blanket is lifted, and the man himself looks down at us. Eyes as cold as a Northeast blizzard.

"Quit what you're doing, you little scum. Chew through that gag and I'll stuff a dirty sock down your throat. My advice, rest yourselves. There's a lot of excitement coming your way!"

He drops the blanket and cackles. "Ain't that right, Pinky?" he asks, raising his voice. "Lots of excitement we got planned."

"Yes, sir. Exciting, to be sure."

Pinky must be the Pinkerton agent, who, apparently, is driving. The eager tone of his voice sends chills through me. Like they can't wait to get started on whatever they have in mind.

I swear, if they touch a hair on my sister's head, I'll explode like a rabid polecat and claw Sydney Barnes with my bare hands. I'll bite him, I'll fight him. I may be small for my age, but I'll do whatever it takes to defend Jo.

Time passes slowly when you're tied up under a smelly blanket, in a space so small and tight it's like being buried alive. I have no idea how long we've been on the road. Thirty minutes? As long as an hour? The Packard has slowed down, and from the sounds and the occasional tooting of a horn, we must be in the city.

The Packard comes to a stop. A window rolls down. Words are exchanged, although I can't make them out exactly. Sounds scrambled, like pig Latin. A Klan password? The window rolls up and the Packard keeps going, quite slowly. Feels like it makes a few turns before it comes to a stop. The engine is killed, doors open, the blanket is whipped off, exposing us to the light of dawn.

Barnes grabs the ropes, hauls us out of the car. Jo lands on her knees. I'm flat on my face in a white gravel driveway, just off a busy avenue.

"Welcome to the Klavern, French fries. Look and be amazed!"

Before us is a vast white building, newly built, taking up most of a wooded lot. Shaped like a barn with a gambrel roof and many windows, but bigger than any barn I've ever seen. Much bigger.

"Half a mile from downtown Portland, with seating for three thousand," Barnes crows. "Every one of them eager to be rid of the likes of you. Come on!"

He drags us inside.

41. *Two Less French Fries*

THE BUILDING LOOKS even larger on the inside, with high-peaked ceilings and a latticework of beams and trusses to hold the whole thing together. Grandstands extend on three sides, with dozens of rows of bench seating facing an enormous stage.

Sydney Barnes jerks at the ropes, knocking us down. "On your knees, you cretins! Bow down to your masters!"

Which strikes me as strange, since we're the only ones in the so-called Klavern. Seeing me look around at the sea of empty benches, Barnes sneers and says, "Thought it best to get you situated before the festivities begin. By sundown every seat will be filled. Come on, Pinky. Lend a hand!"

The Pinkerton drags us to our feet and shoves us

toward the stage. In the center of the stage is a lectern big enough for a giant. Behind the lectern is a curved, white-painted wall and a row of narrow doors. Dressing rooms, Barnes explains. He shoves us through a door into a small, low-ceilinged room equipped with a makeup table and an illuminated mirror.

Does that mean the King Kleagle wears makeup? Not a question I'd dare to ask, even if I didn't have a gag choking me.

The Pinkerton chains us to a heavy steam radiator and yanks the gags out of our mouths. "Not a word. Do not speak unless spoken to, or the gags go back in."

"Very good, Pinky," Barnes says. "The house phone is in the vestibule in the mansion office. We're expecting a call. You know what to say."

"Yes, sir, I do." The Pinkerton tugs the brim of his hat and leaves the room.

Barnes checks the chains that bind us to the radiator and seems satisfied. "Know this: You are powerless. You are pawns, to be traded for an actual human being. I speak of Captain Merriman, the war hero. He had ancestors who fought in the Revolutionary War, and is of pure Anglo-Saxon blood. He's qualified to enlist in our white brotherhood, and if he wishes to keep you alive, that's exactly what he'll do. All that is required is that he stand on our stage and swear to uphold our cause. He'll don the robes and have his photograph taken for the newspapers. 'War hero joins KKK, upholds white race supremacy.'"

"He'll never do it!" Jo snarls.

Barnes laughs. "I get the impression Ray will do pretty much anything Ruthie asks him to do. Our demands have been made. We're awaiting a reply."

"What if he refuses?" Jo wants to know.

Sydney Barnes towers over us, crouched as we are by the radiator. He gives the impression of a man who's enjoying himself, who delights in lashing us with his cruelty. "If Captain Merriman refuses, there will be two less French fries in the world."

He makes the threat so casually, and so coldly, that I gulp in fear. He sounds like he'd almost prefer that alternative. This from a man who joked around with me, who seemed to enjoy my company. All the while he was plotting this: a chance to humiliate us, to threaten us.

He waits for us to say something. He'd love to hear us beg for our lives. Jo doesn't give him the satisfaction. From her haughty attitude, you'd think he was no longer in the dressing room, or had become invisible. She speaks instead to me, softly and in French. *"N'aie pas peur, petit frère, fais confiance d'abord à Dieu, et ensuite à Ruthie Reynard."*

Fear not, little brother. Trust first in God, and second in Ruthie Reynard.

42. *The Wonderful Wizard of Portland, Maine*

SYDNEY BARNES LEAVES us chained to the radiator. He announces that the Klan rally starts at sundown—the better to wave torches and burn crosses—so there's nothing to do but wait and see what happens. Will Captain Merriman agree to their demands? Ruthie has been informed of our abduction, but does she have any idea of our location? Even if she does, how could she take on the three thousand Klansmen who are gathering to celebrate the opening of their new auditorium? Can she rely on the police to help, or has the city police force been infiltrated like the Pinkertons?

All we have are questions with no answers. Which is driving me crazy. Because people who chain kids to radiators are capable of anything. I thrash around, testing the chains, on the verge of panic.

"Davy, all I can do is promise we'll be okay," says Jo, trying to calm me down.

"You can't know that," I protest.

"But I do," she insists. "I can't explain it, but I know in my soul that we'll get out of this alive."

My first reaction is, she's just saying that to ease my fear. Then I remember that my big sister, Josephine, has never lied to me, not even to make me feel better. She always tells the truth, even if it hurts, like the truth about our mama's illness.

I decide to believe her. A huge load goes off my shoulders as the fear ebbs away. Even if we happen to be in mortal danger right at the moment.

Hours go by. We have no food or water, so to distract ourselves from thirst and hunger, we decide to tell each other stories from our favorite books, like we did when we were younger. Mine is *The Magical Land of Noom*. Jo has practically memorized the Oz books, and goes first with *The Wonderful Wizard of Oz*.

"'Dorothy lived in the midst of the great Kansas prairies, with Uncle Henry, who was a farmer, and Aunt Em, who was the farmer's wife . . .'"

"What about Toto? We mustn't forget Toto!"

"I'm getting there. He doesn't come into the story until page three."

She describes the little dog and how he makes Dorothy laugh. When the storm approaches, Jo makes wind-whistling noises, then tells how Toto escapes from Dorothy's arms and hides under the bed. Soon the house is rising into the sky and whirling around, caught in the exact center of the cyclone. Hours pass and Dorothy gets over being afraid and falls asleep and does not wake up until the house drops to the ground with a huge thump.

The way Jo tells it, you can see every detail. The gleam in Toto's eyes. The marvelous beauty of the land of the Munchkins, and the Munchkins themselves, who are about Dorothy's size.

The last thing I remember is the Good Witch giving Dorothy the silver shoes.

———

I'm dreaming about the yellow brick road when Jo awakens me with a gentle shove.

"Davy, somebody is coming!" she hisses.

Footsteps approach.

43. *What Scares Me*

THE NARROW DOOR opens with a bang. Captain Merriman enters in full uniform, as angry as I've ever seen him.

"Unchain these children at once!"

Sydney Barnes sidles into the little room, a hand on the pistol in his belt. "You're not the one giving orders around here, Captain."

"Unchain them or the deal is off!"

Barnes shrugs and takes his own sweet time undoing the chain.

"You left them chained like animals for how many hours, without food or water?" Captain Merriman demands. "What is wrong with you people? Have you no shame?"

Barnes smirks. "We had more important things to

attend to. Like securing your word that you will take the pledge, in exchange for their lives."

"You said they were to be released!"

"Did I? What I meant to say is their lives will be spared, but they will remain under our control. As are you."

"You lying devil!"

The man called Pinky delivers us a plate of sandwiches and a pitcher of water. That seems to calm the captain down, who was on the verge of taking a swing at Barnes, gun or no gun. "Don't eat too fast or it will come back up," he advises us. "Same for the water. Sip slowly."

He crouches down, searching our faces, accessing the damage. He gives my shoulder a squeeze and tries to embrace Jo, but Barnes stops him.

"Stop that!" Barnes shouts. "I said you could see the brats, but you weren't to speak to them until after the ceremony!"

"Oh, shut up," Captain Merriman says. "Jo, Davy, I am so sorry this happened. I'll make it up to you, promise."

Barnes takes the pistol out of his belt and points it. "Out!"

Captain Merriman puts up his hands and backs out of our little room, followed by Sydney Barnes. Through the open door we can see an ocean of white robes filling the stands. A moment later the door is shut and locked from the outside, a sturdy barrel bolt snicking into place. In the center of the door, at eye level (too high for me!) is a round brass disk. Flip it up and you can look through a spy hole to the stage.

"There's thousands of them," Jo says, shaking her head in disgust. "It sickens me that Captain Merriman has to join the Klan to keep us alive."

I drag a footstool to the door so I can look through the spy hole.

The King Kleagle steps to the podium and speaks into an electrified microphone. His voice booms through amplified loudspeakers, filling the auditorium. I'm not going to bother to repeat what he says because it's the same old garbage that he's been spewing since we first heard him. The white race threatened by an invasion of filthy immigrants.

He goes on and on, waving his arms and saluting the crowd. Right arm straight out from the shoulder, fingers splayed, left hand on his heart. The crowd roars approval and chants his name. And no, I'm not sharing that name because the man himself deserves to be forgotten, even as we must never forget what he did and said to poison the minds of so many Mainers.

After about an hour of spouting sewage, he says he has a surprise announcement. The famous war hero, Captain Raymond Merriman, has decided he will no longer fly in the company of lowly immigrants, and has agreed to pledge his allegiance to the Ku Klux Klan.

The cheers become thunderous, deafening. Three thousand Klansmen stamp their feet, shaking the auditorium.

"JOIN US! JOIN US! JOIN US!" they chant.

Captain Merriman steps to the podium. His back is to us, so we can't see his face, but his shoulders are slumped, as if in defeat. He raises his right hand and repeats the Klan pledge, as given to him by the King Kleagle.

Jo looks through the spy hole and groans. "This is our fault. We never should have followed that horrible Sydney to the airfield."

"That was my idea. Blame me."

Flash powder explodes as photographers take pictures of the famous war hero donning a new white satin robe and hood. Like Jo, I feel sick to my stomach. Not because I ate the sandwiches too fast, which I did. No. Because the idea of poor Captain Merriman, dressed as a Klansmen, on the front page of every paper in the state, is so disgusting that it makes me gag. He risked his life in the Great War and has the medals to prove it, and deserves so much better than this!

What Captain Merriman says next shocks me to the core.

"My white brothers, to honor my pledge I will lead a torchlight parade around this great building, and then onto the streets of Portland. Let the city see how many we are! Let them fear and respect us! Follow me, white brothers, follow me!"

What scares me is he sounds like he means it.

44. *Into the Darkness*

"DON'T BE SILLY," Jo says. "The captain a real Klansman? No, he had to be convincing so they won't harm us."

"I don't believe a thing they say."

"Me neither," she says with a sigh.

I watch through the spy hole as Captain Merriman, dressed as a Klansman, strides off the stage with a purpose. The auditorium begins to empty, three thousand white robes heading for the exits, eager to fire up their torches and parade around the building and through the streets of the city, spreading their poisonous hatred.

I'm sure Jo is right about Captain Merriman. Seeing him in that dreadful costume gave me a turn, made me doubt who could be trusted. Sydney Barnes had been kindly and nice right up until the moment he abducted us.

But the captain would never betray us, this I know in my bones.

"We've got to get out of here while we've got the chance."

"I know, Davy, but how?"

I've never heard my big sister sound so discouraged. Looking up, I spot what may be an answer.

"There, Jo. The ceiling vent! Maybe we can pry that out."

"That little thing? It's not big enough for a cat to get through."

"We have to try. If only for Captain Merriman's sake. The only way he gets free of them is for us to escape."

We position a chair beneath the vent. Jo climbs up and manages to slip her fingers through the vent louvers. She pulls down with all her might.

"It won't move!"

"Keep trying!"

She looks down at me. "Pull the chair out from under my feet!"

With the chair taken away, she hangs from the vent with all her weight. Still it does not budge. I grab hold of her legs, lifting my feet from the floor, adding my weight to hers.

Wham!

We're on the floor, legs tangled, and the wrenched-free vent in Jo's triumphant hand.

"We did it!"

I take a moment to catch my breath. Then I reposition the chair under the rectangular opening in the ceiling. Jo is right, it looks barely big enough for a cat to wriggle through, but it is our only chance to escape.

"Boost me," I say, exhaling to make my chest as thin as possible.

"Are you sure?"

"It's our only chance."

Jo stands beside me on the chair and makes a stirrup of her hands. Her eyes are big with concern. She knows how I feel about small spaces, but what choice do we have? With her help, I'm boosted high enough to get my right arm and part of my shoulder through the hole in the ceiling. Exhaling even more, I force my head through the hole, which nearly scrapes my ears off. Ignoring the pain, I reach around blindly with my right hand, and find myself gripping what must be a ceiling joist.

Pulling with all my might, and with Jo pushing from below, I drag my small, skinny body up through the hole and into the darkness.

45. *The Light at the End*

I LIE THERE for a moment, trying to catch my breath in what amounts to an attic crawl space over the dressing rooms. The darkness is broken only by a faint glow from the vent opening. The roof rafters are just above my head, leaving barely enough space to inch along from joist to joist.

My heart is racing. It feels as if a giant fist is squeezing my chest, making me shake and sweat. I'm terrified but what I fear doesn't matter: All that matters is saving Jo. So, get moving, Davy. Don't think about the roof closing in to crush the life out of you. If the KKK return to the hall, there will be no escape.

Faster, Davy, faster. Somewhere a Klansman's watch is ticking.

Gritting my teeth, I pick up the pace, pulling myself

over the space between joists. Take a breath, pull again. Hands raw from the wood. The rough joists scratch at me like splintery fingers. If I can't find a way out, I'm stuck in this narrow, suffocating space. Trapped with no room to turn around. There is no going back. All I can do is drag myself forward.

There has to be a way out!

Funny where your mind will go when you're struggling to survive. One day when I was about nine years old, I came home weeping and trying to hide it, covering my eyes. My dear mother gently pried my hands away, and looked at me with such a force of love—I swear it was like sunshine—that the tears stopped instantly. The other kids in the tenement had been teasing me mercilessly. Of the children my age, I was by far the smallest, and they never let me forget it. Mama knew this, of course, and she also knew that defending me would likely make it worse, because teasing and bullying were as much a way of life as tending the mill machinery.

She hugged me fiercely. "God made you small for a reason," she said. "We may never know His plan, for He works in mysterious ways. One thing I do know," she said, gently placing her hand over my heart, *"ton coeur bat vrai!* Your heart beats true. In your heart you are a giant, a champion! Know that you are always loved, my darling boy, and that will give you courage."

Yes, Mama.

I crawl from joist to joist, rafters scraping the back of my head as I squeeze through an impossibly small crawl space, desperate to find an escape. Saving my sister, that's the only thing that matters. I crawl and crawl, ignoring the pain and fear. Suddenly, wham! My head bumps into a wall. This must be the end of the dressing rooms, and very possibly the end of me.

Discouraged, I lay my head down on the last joist, and that's when I see it. The crawl space makes a ninety-degree turn to the left, and there, not ten feet away, light spills through a grate in the wall.

46. *We Are the Future*

SEEING A WAY out so close at hand is one thing. Getting there is another. It takes a good five minutes to wedge myself to the left an inch at a time, until finally I'm facing in the right direction. I'd love to take a deep breath of relief, but the roof rafters are squeezing the air out of me as it is.

Crawling and wriggling, ignoring the splinters, I inch forward until my fingers touch the grate, which is about a foot and a half wide. I can see through the wooden slats. The great hall is visible below, benches empty as the Klansmen march outside the building.

Please, grate, do not be locked or bolted. Please, please!

I shove the bottom and am astonished as it opens easily, hinged at the top. Wriggling through, I tumble to the empty stage, landing on my back and rolling. The fall knocks the air out of me, but I don't care.

I did it! I run to the dressing room door directly behind the podium and slide the sturdy bolt. Jo swings the door open instantly and throws her arms around me.

"Davy, you made it! I was so worried you got stuck." She leans away, inspecting me. "What are all these scratches?"

"Never mind that." I grab her hand. "This way!"

We hurry out to the abandoned stage and down the steps. We duck under the stands, out of view of any stragglers, and run along the great beamed wall. At the back of the building we come upon an open exit door and peer around the edge.

Thousands of Klansmen on the march, in a parade of white robes and burning torches.

"They're all headed the other way," I whisper, heart in my throat. "Now's our chance."

We race up a grassy hillside and into a small stand of trees overlooking the back of the giant barn, where we can see but not be seen.

At least twenty Klansmen are patrolling the perimeter of the estate, armed with shotguns and baseball bats. The moon isn't quite up yet, but hundreds of blazing torches illuminate the night, driving back the shadows. Led by Captain Merriman and the King Kleagle, the roaring, chanting Klansmen march six abreast around the giant barn.

"WHITE RACE, MASTER RACE! WHITE RACE, MASTER RACE! K! K! K! K! K! K!"

What really hurts isn't the hateful words; it's knowing that under those hoods are dairy farmers and fishermen, doctors and lawyers, machinists and salesmen. The folks who live next door and look you square in the eye when they say "good day." While inside they want you gone; they wish you were never born.

"WHITE RACE, MASTER RACE! WHITE RACE, MASTER RACE! K! K! K! K! K! K!"

When you study a photograph of the hood-and-robe costume, it might look almost comical. Take it from me, when thousands are marching and chanting their hateful message, directed at you and people like you, it is nothing less than terrifying. These individual men, these fellow citizens, have become a raging mob. They are no longer thinking; they are a beast seething with anger and resentment.

"Remember, of all the things they hate, they hate the future most," Jo says.

"I thought they hated us."

"That's what I'm saying, little brother," Jo says,

giving my shoulders a squeeze. "We *are* the future."

We're about to make a run for it, to try to slip away into one of the side streets, when a noise stops us.

The sound of propellers approaching in the night.

47. *What Fire Loves*

OF ALL THE death-defying stunts I witnessed in our season with the flying circus, this is the most amazing of them all. Two moonlit biplanes racing above Forest Avenue at full speed, at an altitude of barely fifty feet. Ruthie's Jenny and Elsie's *Liberty Belle*. Zooming skillfully between buildings, and just above the trees that line the avenue, they bank without slowing. Aiming themselves at the throngs of torch-bearing Klansmen.

The biplanes buzz the crowd, so close the torchlight illuminates the fabric-covered wings. In the resulting panic, hundreds of men drop their torches and flee.

The march has turned into chaos as the biplanes keep buzzing the crowd. Fire spreads from the dropped torches, burning up the lawn and much of the dry shrubbery that surrounds the giant barn. Many of the men have pulled off their hoods, the better to see their way clear of the airborne attack. Their faces look wild and confused, but one thing is clear: They fear the whirring propellers.

"FIRE! FIRE!"

Behind us the night air quivers and booms with a wave of heat. Great flames rise as the brush fire spreads into the Klavern building. The new pine construction ignites like a match head, and soon flames are blazing through the windows and up into the roof.

We have to get away before the flames ignite the trees we're sheltering behind.

"Over there!" I shout. "Go! Go!"

We run like the wind, heading for an area the Klan has deserted. The men guarding the property have left to help fight the fire.

"*Da questa parte!* This way!"

I know that voice! In the street at the bottom of the hill, Tony Martini is waving his arms to attract our attention. Behind him is Ruthie's Cadillac, ready for escape.

Tony scoops us up into one great bear hug. "Where is captain?" he wants to know.

The answer soon appears in person, ripping off his

Klan robe. Smelling heavily of smoke, he drops to his knees to embrace us. "Thank the good Lord. I thought you perished in the fire."

Jo tells him how we escaped.

The captain applauds our ingenuity. "We had a plan for your rescue, but we didn't expect that in their panic they'd burn down their own Klavern. When I saw what was happening, I ran back into the building, fearing the worst. And here you are, safe and sound! Davy, what you did, that was brave and brilliant. You saved two lives today. Thank you!"

He embraces us again, heaving a huge sigh.

"Oh, Captain Merriman, we're so sorry you had your picture taken in that horrible robe. It's not fair!" Jo bursts out.

"Not your fault," he says. "Don't worry, we've got a plan for that, too. Let's get out of here!"

We tumble into the back seat of the Cadillac. Tony blasts the horn three times. He waits a beat, then sounds the horn three more times.

"That's the signal that you're safe," the captain explains.

Sure enough, the biplanes waggle their wings in response. They veer off and away, climbing to altitude in the moonlit sky. As we flee in the Cadillac, fire equipment begins to arrive. Men in helmets and rubber coats spill from trucks, rushing to the scene with fire axes in hand.

Good luck. What fire loves most is newly sawn pine, rich with sap.

48. *A Good Newspaper Never Sleeps*

THE CAPTAIN DIRECTS Tony to the Portland police headquarters, where we report the abduction. The wary desk sergeant doesn't exactly leap into action, but he promises to investigate Sydney Barnes and the man he calls Pinky.

They're never arrested, having fled the state.

From the police station, we go to the nearly new *Portland Press Herald* building. It's very late, but the lights are on on all seven floors.

"Night shift," Captain Merriman explains. "A good newspaper never sleeps."

Ruthie is waiting for us in the lobby. The captain rushes to embrace her, and even Ruthie, brave and daring Ruthie, pauses to brush tears of relief from her cheeks.

"Oh, my darling, we must make this right," she says.

We are greeted in the lobby by the paper's editor in chief. The name on the masthead, he explains with a rueful laugh.

"That's how they chain me to my desk," he says, blinking behind round spectacles. "With a promise of fame and fortune. Fame is my name in every edition of the paper, and fortune is barely enough to keep the wolf from the door."

"That sounds terrible!" Jo exclaims.

"Ha! Wouldn't trade it for the world! Telling the truth, one word at a time, that is its own reward. Come, sit, tell me your story. I've been warned it's rather amazing."

49. *Our Last Happy Day*

WAR HERO SACRIFICES HONOR TO SAVE ABDUCTED KIDS
FLYING CIRCUS TO THE RESCUE!
ATTACK FROM AIR ROUTS KLAN CELEBRATION

Those are only a few of the headlines from articles that ran, not only in Portland, Maine, but nationwide. Most readers seem to agree that Captain Merriman did the right thing, pretending to join the Klan, and that he should not be held to his pledge of loyalty.

"No man should be held to an oath obtained under duress" is how the editor of the *Press Herald* put it, in an opinion piece supporting the captain and condemning the Klan in no uncertain terms.

In the end, bringing the Maine Klan down takes a lot more than an editorial, or our small efforts to embarrass the hate-mongers. Headlines can't stop haters from hating. Only weeks after the events at the Portland Klavern, the Klan helps elect a governor sympathetic to their ideas of white supremacy and the reviling of Blacks and immigrants. The efforts to mainstream intolerance and hatred will continue until the organization finally collapses under a financial scandal some years later.

———

The captain fired the Pinkertons and has hired new security guards. Men he knows personally, from his time in the army. The situation is temporary, as we have only one more venue before the season is over.

Ruthie and her friend and aviation rival, Elsie Bell, will be competing in a loop-the-loop contest at the Farmington Fair. Ruthie currently holds the record at ninety-two loops in a row, and Elsie has announced her intention to shatter that record by achieving a hundred loops in a row.

The next morning Ruthie and Elsie are still talking about the nighttime air raid on Klan headquarters, and the thrill of their low-level attack.

"When Ruthie told me what she had in mind, I did not hesitate. What a thrill it was to buzz the Klan headquarters—and what a sight to see it burn! Proves those Klansmen can't be trusted with matches, let alone torches."

We're at the train station, awaiting the arrival of Ruthie's special railway car, which will be transporting the circus to Farmington.

Riding in the plush, private railway car is always a thrill. Despite what Ruthie said that day we dropped the stink bomb, flying doesn't appeal to me. Whereas, after our experience at the *Portland Press Herald*, I can easily imagine myself working for a newspaper, making sure the truth gets printed. Putting black ink on white paper seems like a worthy occupation, if ever I get the chance.

I began this adventure without a clue as to where life might take me. Now I have some notion of the way forward.

———

Our trip to Farmington is especially pleasant because the entire crew of the circus is along for the ride. For this one last trip of the season, all the circus vehicles are being transported by rail. At one end of the car the men are playing cards and laughing uproariously. Not being much of a card player, I stick with my sister and the ladies, listening to stories of Ruthie's exploits, as recounted by Elsie, who seems to know enough about Ruthie Reynard to write a book on the subject.

"She wouldn't dare!" Ruthie responds when I raise the possibility.

"Never fear," Elsie says with a laugh. "I barely have the patience to answer my mail, let alone write a biography."

Jo has been especially quiet, as if content to simply be in the presence of those she so admires. It's not until Elsie asks about her wing-dance act that she breaks her silence and joins in the conversation.

Later, we break out the Victrola, crank it up, and play the famous song. Elsie is soon following Jo, bouncy step for bouncy step. Then Ruthie jumps in, and wouldn't you know it, she's equally adept. Soon we're all clapping to the rhythm and singing along, even Mrs. Mangano, who has a lovely voice. The dancers tap heels to hands, do that funny bit crossing their knees together. Dancing forward, dancing back, waving their hands, and laughing all the while.

Joy fills the railway car. It's our last happy day.

50. *What Falls from the Pale Blue Sky*

AUTUMN HAS COME to the Farmington fairgrounds. The particular kind of autumn day when you can feel both the last warm breeze of summer and the chill of the coming winter. The foliage is a blaze of glory so vivid it almost hurts to look, but look you must, and be amazed. The sky is the palest blue, decorated with a few thin clouds.

Smoke from the sausage grills wafts into the stands, rousing the hungry.

"Popcorn! Hey, popcorn!"

I can barely keep up with demand.

Our air show starts the usual way, with little Donkey Boy at the wheel of the speeding race car. After taking my bow, and drinking up the applause, I realize how much I'll miss this, making people laugh and applaud. To be honest, the costume is getting tighter and harder to wriggle into. Like it or not, I'm outgrowing the role.

Next up is Patrice at the wheel of the racing Bugatti and Tony Martin leaping from the car to a rope ladder dangling from Captain Merriman's biplane. He climbs the rope, slips into the front cockpit, and first-time spectators assume the stunt is over. Many are shocked and thrilled when he climbs out to the wing and then down to the landing gear, where he hangs upside down for the hat trick.

The dangerous stunt goes off without incident. The crowd roars its approval.

"LADIES AND GENTLEMEN AND CHILDREN OF ALL AGES. CAST YOUR EYES TO THE EAST. YOU ARE ABOUT TO WITNESS AN ASTONISHING DISPLAY OF AGILITY FROM WING DANCER JOSEPHINE MICHAUD. PLEASE WELCOME THE AMAZING JOSEPHINE."

The band erupts into that famous song and my sister executes that famous dance flawlessly.

"JO-SEPH-INE! JO-SEPH-INE!"

I confess, I'm chanting along with the crowd, delighted Jo has one last triumph before the season closes. Where shall we be a week from now? I can't help wondering. The circus crew is about to disperse. Where does that leave Jo and me? Where will we live? Will we stay together? Will

Ruthie arrange for someone to look after us? Questions I'm almost afraid to ask.

"Popcorn! Hey, popcorn!"

I sell out all the paper sacks in the carrier and am about to return to Maggie's kettle when Elsie's speedy Curtiss R-6 comes roaring over the horizon.

"LADIES AND GENTLEMEN AND CHILDREN OF ALL AGES. CAST YOUR EYES TO THE SOUTH! WELCOME THE FASTEST FEMALE IN THE WORLD, MISS ELSIE BELL, PILOTING HER CURTISS R-6!"

Elsie zooms over the stands, waving gaily, her scarf streaming. Today's contest will not require speed so much as skill.

I tell myself to stop fretting and be grateful for all the circus has given me. Especially the gift of friendship. Ruthie, Maggie, the captain, Tony and Patrice, and now Elsie Bell. How many boys my age ever come in contact with such a selection of daring heroes?

"CAST YOUR EYES TO THE WEST! WELCOME AVIATRIX RUTHIE REYNARD, WHO WILL BE COMPETING IN A LOOP-THE-LOOP CONTEST WITH MISS BELL! THE WINNER WILL DOUBTLESS SET A NEW WORLD RECORD."

Ruthie's biplane zooms low. She gives a thumbs-up sign as she passes the grandstand. She and Elsie then join in formation and prepare for the contest. They fly in parallel, gradually widening the gap between planes.

At a signal from Ruthie, the two aircraft execute a steep climb. At the very top of the loop they invert, flying upside down as they start the dive that will complete the loop.

The crowd screams. Something has fallen from the R-6, which begins to spin out of control.

It is Elsie Bell, falling to her death.

51. *The End, or Maybe Not*

FROM THAT TERRIBLE moment, a dark and all-consuming grief descends upon the flying circus. Ruthie has kept the vow she made at the beginning of the season: that if any fatal accident should occur on her watch, she would quit on the spot.

She has done so. The flying circus is no more.

Our last act is to transport Elsie Belinski's coffin home by train, from Farmington, Maine, to Lynn, Massachusetts. The private railway car has never been so somber, filled as it is with our soon-to-be-dispersed circus crew. Tony weeps openly and talks of retiring from the business of risking his life every day.

"Così giovane!" he exclaims. "So young!"

He may go back to Italy, to visit family, taking time to decide what to do next. Patrice has already received an offer from a regular big-top circus, which values his skills as a tumbler. Mrs. Mangano will be returning to Brooklyn, New York, where a famous Italian restaurant has long wanted her to command their kitchen.

"I miss you!" she says, giving each of us a kiss on the cheek. "I miss all of you! Never will I forget you! Never!"

As leader of our group, Ruthie has taken the loss of her young rival the hardest of all. She is inconsolable. The captain attempts to comfort her by explaining that the terrible accident was not her fault. Nor was it an act of sabotage by some agent of the Klan, seeking revenge.

"I examined the wreckage," he says. "Her shoulder harness was undamaged. It was simply not fastened correctly, and the buckle popped open at exactly the wrong moment. It was a mistake, a terrible mistake."

"I will not blame her!"

"No one is to blame, my darling."

It is one thing to read newspaper articles about daredevils perishing in fatal accidents, which happens with shocking frequency. Quite another when it happens to one of our own.

Jo has scarcely spoken a word since that terrible moment. Even so, I get the impression she will never again dance upon wings. The joy she took in that is no longer possible, not for her.

"Whatever happens, we'll be okay," I assure her. "Normally you're the one who says that. Today it's my turn."

"Oh, Davy!"

It feels like something happened to me over the course of what was, up until yesterday, a time filled with excitement, adventure, and so many new experiences I can hardly keep track. Over those months, I've grown. Not only physically—I'm a half inch taller!—but in how I look at the world, and who I might be when I grow up.

What was it the editor said about telling the truth, one word at a time? Maybe I can do something like that, something that makes a difference, pushing back against the hatred.

I decide then and there that if I have to finish school at an orphanage, so be it, I won't complain, not if Jo can visit me now and then.

After our sad stop in Elsie's hometown, Maggie, Tony, and Patrice continue on to Boston, to embark on their separate journeys. Our railway car is guided onto a northern track, destination Portland, Maine.

When we are at last underway, Ruthie tells Jo and me that she has an announcement to make. Before she continues, Ray Merriman takes her hand. His eyes are full of Ruthie as she speaks.

"Life is simply too precious to waste. We each have our time upon the earth and I want to cherish every moment given me." She takes a deep breath, smiling bravely. "Captain Merriman and I wanted you to know we intend to be married as soon as it can be arranged."

Jo claps her hands together. "How wonderful! Congratulations!"

"Me too," I say. "I mean, what Jo said."

Ruthie hugs us, and then stands back. "You will of course be in the wedding party. But we have another, much more important request. Ray?"

The captain removes his hat and makes a little bow in our direction. "Josephine Mary Michaud, David Louis Michaud, would you do us the honor of allowing us to legally adopt you? We not only want to get married, we want to have a family, and as far as we're concerned, you're it."

Jo and I look at each other, in shock and surprise. Not that there's any question about the answer.

"Yes, please!"

Do not think this a happy ending, dear readers. It is, truly, a happy beginning.

Epilogue

A Lifetime Later

ALTHOUGH MEMBERSHIP IN the Klan itself has declined, the idea of white supremacy still exists in Maine, as it does just about everywhere. New organizations promoting hate have sprung up worldwide. Those who believe in equality and democracy must continue to speak out against intolerance, with love for all in our hearts, including those who hold such repugnant beliefs.

In case you're curious about what happened to us, Jo went on to college and became a much beloved schoolteacher in Cape Elizabeth, a job she cherished. I asked her once if she missed the thrill of being a daredevil, and she said there's nothing so thrilling as teaching a child to read. That's my Jo. Along the way she married happily, became a mother of four, and eventually grandmother and great-grandmother and matriarch to an entire clan.

As for me, after finishing high school I took a job as a copy boy at the *Portland Press Herald*, running stories between desks. I must have liked the place, because I eventually rose to be a reporter, then city editor, then editor in chief, and finally publisher. Oh, and I wrote a few books along the way.

I won't mention all the awards I won because I'm much too modest. Ha!

This book is for the Amazing Josephine, on the occasion of her one hundredth birthday, which she celebrates in good health and with a clear mind. Remember, Jo, that summer when we were orphans, and we joined a flying circus? That often-wonderful, sometimes-terrible season when you danced on wings, and bad men roamed the earth? They owned their hatred, but we owned the sky.

You were my big sister and my fearless hero, then and now.

With all my love,
Davy

Information You May Find Interesting

Readers often want to know where authors get ideas. In this case, from two places. An old seaman's chest and a family tale. The chest contained many albums of black-and-white photographs taken mostly by my grandfather, who died suddenly when my father was twelve years old, at the height of the Great Depression. Some of the most fascinating photos are of a then-famous female aviator, Ruth Law, who happened to be my grandfather's first cousin. Ruth was a daredevil. She founded a flying circus in her name and toured the country for more than four years.

I never met Ruth, but she and her older brother, daredevil and movie stuntman Rodman Law, were two of my childhood heroes. I've been searching for a way to put Ruth and her flying circus in a story for years. It was a

Ruth Law and her daredevils

family tale that helped me find a way. It was such a strange and shocking story that for a long time I assumed it had been wildly exaggerated. I now know it to be fundamentally true.

As a young man, my grandfather worked for a time in Chicago. When he came back home to Rye Beach, New Hampshire, he brought with him a young Irish Catholic bride, my nana, Jean Glazier. One night soon after they arrived, Klansmen on horseback surrounded the house, carrying torches and setting fire to a burning cross. My great-grandfather William Isaac Philbrick, renowned for his skills with a shotgun, chased the Klansmen off the property, identifying several of them because he recognized their horses.

The Ku Klux Klan in lily-white New England, in the 1920s, how could that possibly be? Out of curiosity, I began to do some research, and soon discovered that membership in an immigrant-hating, Northern version of the Klan had exploded throughout New England in that time period. Worst hit was Maine, a bastion of old Yankees. The intention was to make their twisted beliefs part of mainstream thinking, and for a time, they succeeded. At the height of their hate-mongering, a hundred and fifty thousand residents of Maine were dues-paying members of the Ku Klux Klan. In 1924, they helped elect a governor.

There being few Blacks to terrorize in Maine, these avowed white supremacists focused their intolerance on a recent influx of immigrants who had come to Maine to work the mills. French Canadian, Italian, Polish, Russian, Jews—all were deemed to be "lower races" by a Klan intent on promoting white racial purity. Much of the language and ideology used to advance their ideas was later taken up by Nazi propagandists, and continues to this day in hate organizations spawned by the original Klan.

I am indebted to Mark Paul Richard, whose book *Not a Catholic Nation: The Ku Klux Klan Confronts New England in the 1920s* started me on my journey, and to Kelly J. Baker for her book *Gospel According to the Klan: The KKK's Appeal to Protestant America, 1915–1930*, which helped me understand how the men in white hoods came to believe what they believed. Linda Gordon's *The Second Coming of the KKK: The Ku Klux Klan of the 1920s and the American Political Tradition* provided a timely and vivid context for the events in *We Own the Sky*. Thanks to you all.

Although some of the scenes are based on events that actually happened—there really was a huge Klan Klavern in Portland, Maine, and it really did burn—my story is fiction. I made a lot of it up, and any historical inaccuracies are my own.

Additional Reading

Young readers interested in Ruth Law and her exploits will enjoy the highly informative *Fearless Flyer: Ruth Law and Her Flying Machine*, by Heather Lang, beautifully illustrated by Raúl Colón.

About the Author

Newbery Honor author Rodman Philbrick grew up on the coast of New Hampshire and has been writing novels since the age of sixteen. Eventually he turned to the genre of adult mystery-and-suspense thrillers and published his first novel at the age of twenty-eight.

Freak the Mighty, Philbrick's first book for young readers, was published by Scholastic. Now considered a classic, it has sold more than five million copies and was made into a movie, *The Mighty*. Philbrick wrote a sequel, *Max the Mighty*, because "so many kids wrote to me suggesting ideas for a sequel that I decided I'd better write one myself before someone else did."

Philbrick's rip-roaring historical novel about an inveterate teller of tall tales, *The Mostly True Adventures of Homer P. Figg*, was set during the Civil War, and was chosen as a 2010 Newbery Honor Book. The Kennedy Center commissioned a theatrical production, which premiered in 2012. Another novel that examines American history is *Zane and the Hurricane: A Katrina Story*, about Zane Dupree and his dog, Bandit, who are trapped in New Orleans just as Hurricane Katrina hits the city. This dramatic survival tale is both heroic and poignant, educating readers about an unforgettable catastrophe.

Wildfire, a 2019 Book Fairs selection, is a thrilling story set in the tinder-dry forests of Maine. *School Library Journal*'s starred review called it "an intense tale of survival and action."

Wild River, published in 2021, sends readers rushing down a raging river on a life-or-death adventure when a white water rafting trip goes terribly wrong.

Philbrick engages young readers with stories about ordinary children who are suddenly faced with seemingly insurmountable obstacles—and must summon up courage they don't even know they have. For this ability to connect with readers, Rodman Philbrick's books have been given awards and nominations by more than thirty-five states—often multiple times.